A Bait of Perjury

A Novel of Suspense and Legal Intrigue

By

WALLACE SAVAGE

A
GENESIS PRESS
BOOK

Published By
DROKE HOUSE, PUBLISHERS
Anderson, S. C.
***

Distributed By
Grosset & Dunlap
51 Madison Avenue, New York

A BAIT OF PERJURY
Copyright © 1970 By Wallace Savage

FIRST EDITION

Standard Book Number: 8375-6755-6
Library of Congress Catalog Card Number: 71-123353
Manufactured In The United States of America
Book Design By Bill Earle
Published By
DROKE HOUSE Publishers Inc.
Anderson, S. C.

To two people whose patience is remarkable:
my wife, Dorothy,
and
my teacher, Dwight Swain

Chapter 1

Even when it's hot as hell, it looks cool in that rolling, tree-covered country of east Texas that the natives call the Piney Woods. Green with pine and blue-stem grass, dotted with rivers and lakes, this pleasant land gave forth an illusion of coolness even on a blistering August afternoon with the sun hot and high enough to drive a salamander indoors.

All the same, except for one impatient man, on this hot Monday in August no one around Pinewood's town square seemed energized by the illusion. Shades were closed against the heat on most of the one- and two-story buildings that fronted the courthouse square. The handful of elderly, overalled men in front of Lone Star Drug and Bus Depot sprawled listlessly on the sidewalk benches.

Next door two tanned farmers in khaki trousers and high-topped work boots made a languid inspection of the second-hand power saw on display in front of Hank Neilson's hardware store.

But in the entry next to Neilson's a man in his late twenties stood tense and fidgeting, a seersucker coat over his arm. Every few minutes he stepped into the glare of the August sun to stare up and down the street. Then, returning to the shade of the doorway, he balanced restlessly on the balls of his feet.

Above him, on the middle of the three windows facing the square, large gilt letters spelled out "Holt Lawson, Lawyer". Below, a wooden sign with the same wording hung over the doorway about which the man hovered.

At each impatient jiggle, the young man's close-cropped, thick black hair brushed the bottom of the sign. When for a moment he stood resting his arms against the sides of the door, the breadth of his shoulders made the entry seem designed for a smaller breed.

Once more he stepped out onto the sidewalk and scanned the street. With the thumb and forefinger of his right hand he tugged nervously at the little bump in his nose that threw an otherwise handsome profile out of kilter.

Now a flash of sun glinting on metal disturbed the shade of the oak trees. The man turned toward the huge three-story red sandstone affair that was Pinewood County's courthouse.

One of the heavy iron entrance doors swung open. A tall, dark-haired girl in a white linen suit stepped out and looked around. The man waved.

The girl came across the lawn at once, her long legs stretching the skirt of her linen suit at each stride.

The impatient young man slung his seersucker coat over his shoulder, trotted across the street and met her in the thick shade of an oak.

"What's up, Burgess?" he demanded. "Did you hear from Doc?"

"Not from Doc, Holt; but I've heard from Judge Woodruff every five minutes. He sent me to tell you to stop stalling while you wait for Doc and put on your other witnesses."

Frowning, Holt tugged again at the bridge of his nose. "My only other witness is Shelton, and I'm saving him for my clincher. When he tells that jury why Reg is trying to get Adelaide put away, they'd bring in a verdict of 'sound mind'

6

even if the whole American Board of Psychiatry said she was nutty as a pecan harvest."

"Then you go sit in the courtroom and let me watch for Doc." Burgess brushed back a damp lock of hair. "Honestly, Holt, it isn't just that eye of Woodruff's sending chills down my back. The jury's getting fretful."

Holt glared up and down the deserted street. "I'm not going to get stampeded into calling my plays in the wrong order," he declared. "If I let the best client I have wind up in the booby hatch, nobody'd hire me to bail a drunk out of city jail."

Burgess managed a quick smile, but the brown of her eyes deepened with worry. She turned back toward the courthouse.

"Wait a minute," Holt said. "I'll go face old Glass-eye."

Just then a car with the single word "Taxi" on the side turned into the square. It carried a gray-haired passenger with a stubby pipe in his mouth.

Holt gave Burgess's arm a squeeze and spun her around.

"Go tell 'em Doc's here!" he exulted and trotted back to the street.

The taxi pulled into the curb. The gray-haired man got out, tall and lean, and stood blinking at the brightness. Taking the pipe from his mouth in long, wiry fingers, with deft movements he knocked it empty against the sole of his shoe, hesitated, started to stick the briar away in the pocket of his brown tweed coat, then instead pulled out a tobacco pouch.

"Put that hayburner away!" Holt hooked his hand under Dr. Hardwick's arm and pushed. "We've got to get up to court."

The corners of Doc's thin lips turned down. He twisted his slender, sensitive features into an expression of extreme distaste. "All right. Let's get it over with."

7

He dropped pouch and pipe into his coat pocket as he spoke. But he moved only as fast as Holt shoved him toward the red stone courthouse, up the wide blue granite stairs and between the thick marble columns of the south entrance.

In the dim hall Dr. Hardwick pulled his arm free and continued under his own power. "Dammit, Holt," he said. "I'd rather be wheeled into an operating room than go on that witness stand. There I'd at least have an anaesthetic."

Holt chuckled. "It's not that I *want* to run you through the wringer, Doc. But those head shrinkers Kane sprang on me put on quite a performance."

The old man muttered something incoherent. In the elevator, he sagged into one of the corners and took hold of the elbow-high railing. The muscles of his mouth drew tight, squeezing out the blood and whitening his lips.

Holt punched the button. "Relax, Doc," he said. "All you do is take a couple of minutes to tell the simple truth about Adelaide's condition. Everybody in the county knows and trusts you. You'll blow those quacks sky-high."

Doc bent his head. The wrinkled hands that touched the railing shook visibly.

Holt frowned. "I've told you . . . if you'd let Adelaide get on that stand for five minutes, you wouldn't have to testify."

"Now don't start that again!" Dr. Hardwick snapped, head up once more. "If it takes me to put the quietus to this damn lunacy suit, let's get on with it. Adelaide's heart can't take the stress, and that's final.

"Okay, okay," Holt soothed. "I just thought . . . Adelaide says all she has to do is pop one of those pills under her tongue, and she's all right."

"Adelaide may be a business genius, but she's no doctor. It's not those angina attacks that worry me. They're just pains caused by the heart not getting enough blood. The pills dilate the blood vessels and fix that. What worries me is that

8

those angina attacks are a warning – can lead to an honest-to-God heart attack."

"You're the doctor," Holt conceded and began to prepare for the courtroom.

First he slipped his seersucker coat on over his short-sleeved shirt and tightened his blue four-in-hand tie; Judge Woodruff tolerated no casual dress by lawyers. Then he extracted a ball point pen from his coat and tried poking out the point, making sure it wouldn't work. Satisfied that the pen was out of whack, he carefully secured it in his inside pocket.

The elevator jarred to a stop at the third floor. Holt led the way down the hall and through the handful of men standing just inside the courtroom door.

Judge Woodruff leaned across his elevated bench, absorbed in conversation with two strangers whose natty business suits and expensive briefcases marked them as out-of-town lawyers. Holt braced himself for a nasty look from the ghastly, whitish left eye which Woodruff reserved for glares of castigation. But the judge continued to regard the strangers through his right eye – a limpid, friendly, mildly curious brown orb. The left still stared into space as though uninterested in the proceedings.

Relieved, Holt nodded for Doc to follow, then made his way inside the oak railing that marked the area reserved for those with business before the court. He headed for the long table in front of the judge's bench.

Reg and Kane already were seated on the opposition's side of the table. Holt's efforts to slip his witness past them failed. Both got to their feet the moment Doc appeared.

Holt turned back. He wasn't worried about Reg. The red-haired little toady couldn't change Doc's testimony with that personality smile the girls went for.

But, considering Doc's condition, Holt didn't want the

9

old man alone with Kane for even a moment. He'd seen Kane tower over a skittish witness, fix him with those piercing blue eyes, and reduce the guy to jellyfish state before the first question and answer.

Holt got back to the group just in time to hear Reg ask solicitiously, "How's Aunt Adelaide?"

"She's great," Holt snapped, before Doc had a chance to answer. "She just loves her precious Reggie's trying to get her tossed in the nuthouse."

As he spoke, Holt put his hand under Doc's arm. Guiding the older man around the table, he got them seated with himself between Burgess and Doc.

The tension eased. Holt started to turn his attention back to the group at the bench . . . then stopped short and did a double-take.

Somehow, Burgess had shed her working-girl look. The green silk blouse she wore revealed a disturbing amount of olive skin, evenly tanned. It glowed in a very unsecretarial way.

Instinctively Holt turned to catch any jury reaction, good or bad. The jurors returned carefully neutral looks that told him they hadn't made up their minds about the case or were against him. None of them seemed to be eyeing Burgess with disapproval.

Still Holt pondered. What the devil had the gal done to herself during recess? Not that Burgess ever was anything you'd throw rocks at. But before recess she'd looked so — well, so functional.

A moment's study and he pinpointed the issue — a tiny thing to have made such a radical change.

Giving in to the heat, Burgess had slipped off the coat of her white linen suit; and, without the coat, the issue became one of what her blouse *didn't* do. Specifically, it didn't conceal her shapely bronzed arms. Or camouflage the contours of her round, firm breasts.

Holt shrugged. Nothing to do about it now. Only . . . he repressed a sigh . . . it was too bad Kane had scratched every prospective juror who lived in Pinewood. A Pinewood man could have set the rest right that Burgess functioned only as a coldly efficient transcribing machine, regardless of what she looked like, as the same Pinewood man could have told them that Adelaide Bailey was crazy like a fox.

A couple of sharp raps sounded at the front of the courtroom. Holt turned toward the judge's bench.

"I've just set an important matter for Wednesday morning." Judge Woodruff's wall-eye swept the courtroom, daring anyone to object. Then, the pallid left eye fixed on Holt. "I see no reason why you gentlemen can't finish your evidence and arguments by tomorrow afternoon if we have no more undue delay."

Holt got the message: stop stalling. No reply was necessary because the judge hadn't asked anybody anything. Instead he'd laid down the law.

Leaning forward, Holt started to nudge Doc toward the witness stand.

Now, however, quite unnecessarily, Matthew Kane shoved his great frame out of his chair and straightened to his full six foot four, demanding the attention of the court.

Holt tensed. Heads up, he warned himself. Kane had stolen more than one case with sharp practice.

Judge Woodruff made an impatient gesture with his gavel; looked inquiringly at Kane.

Facing more toward the jurors than the judge, the big lawyer attracted their attention with a senatorial gesture of running his fingers through his long, iron-gray hair. The cold blue eyes warmed suddenly with an inner light that Kane seemed able to switch on at will. His powerful, sonorous voice carried easily to the six men in the jury box. "May it

11

please the Court, the Bible says, 'use not vain repetitions'. I'm confident I need put up no more witnesses."

"Let's see how confident the old shyster is after I put on Doc and Shelton," Holt rasped to Burgess.

He could almost feel her stiffen. She gripped his arm with a hand that trembled slightly. "Remember, Holt, don't let him get your goat," she pleaded.

Holt scowled at the other lawyer's frock-length alpaca coat and faultless black string bow tie. "Last of the old school of legal giants!" he snorted. "Bible-quoting hypocrite! How does he get by with it?"

"Holt . . ."

Holt shrugged away her hand. "I'll play it cool." He stood briefly, "I call Dr. Alexander Hardwick."

Doc winced, looked about as happy as a condemned man denied a last minute reprieve, and tottered to the stand. Judge Woodruff exacted the usual oath that witness's testimony would be the truth, the whole truth, and nothing but the truth.

Dr. Hardwick agreed and turned to Holt with a guarded look. Holt swore under his breath. Scared, Doc was the picture of a man about to lie like a trooper.

"State your name, please." Holt said.

"Dr. Alexander Hardwick." Doc's relief at knowing the answer to the question was evident.

Taking it slowly, gradually building up Doc's confidence, Holt proceeded to qualify him as an expert witness. Doc's Scotch parents had sent him back to Edinburgh for medical training. He had returned to Pinewood to go into general practice. Yes, he had had opportunity to observe Adelaide Bailey. Been her doctor for thirty years.

Holt watched the jurors as he put the questions. The lanky fellow in the chair nearest the judge followed Doc's testimony intently. The small, nervous brunette next to him

12

copied. But the two jurors in the middle divided their attention between Doc and some topic of their own. At the end, the stubbiest of the group had his hands folded over his stomach, and his eyelids drooped as though he had used the coffee break to bolt something a bit more solid.

A thick law book lay conveniently near Holt's briefcase. He pulled the case against it. The legal tome hit the floor with a satisfactory crash. Looking apologetic, Holt recovered the volume, stayed on his feet and moved to the end of the jury box farthest from the witness stand.

If the noise of the book hadn't shaken the drowsy juror awake, Holt saw to it that the volume of his voice would. "Now, Dr. Hardwick, based upon that long observation of Adelaide Bailey, state whether in your opinion she is of sound or unsound mind."

"She's absolutely sound mentally!"

It was Doc's most positive answer so far. Holt decided it was a good time to cut it off. He turned to Matthew Kane. "Your witness," he snapped, and returned to his seat.

Kane rose slowly and walked to the witness stand. For a few moments he just stood there with his cold blue eyes drilling down into the doctor. Holt could feel the jury tensing, waiting for the attack. Dr. Hardwick licked his lips.

Hating Kane, Holt admitted to himself that this ramrod-straight giant knew all the tricks.

"You've seen that horseless carriage Miss Bailey has herself driven around town in, haven't you?" Kane demanded.

"Of course." Doc was instantly defensive. "Man from Dallas offered her a fortune for it."

"Yes, but she used it all through the years when it wasn't worth a cent, didn't she?"

Holt penciled himself a note. "Built Adelaide's Breads Inc. into a giant corporation while driving junk heap."

13

Kane was taking the course Holt wanted. Now, when Holt had Doc on redirect examination, he'd hammer away at the fact that Adelaide's idiosyncrasies were long-standing — nothing new brought on by old age. And that she'd amassed a fortune while enjoying them. Which, Mr. Kane, would be the last thing the jury would have in mind from Doc's testimony!

Kane pressed on. "Now tell me, doctor, has Adelaide Bailey bought a new dress in fifty years?"

"Well, Adelaide's kind of eccentric there. Has her clothes made. Dresses the way she did as a young woman."

Holt dittoed the "amassed a fortune," chuckled, and added "while dressing like Kane does."

But it seemed a good time to give Doc some relief. Holt pressed down on his pencil, breaking the point. Reaching inside his coat pocket, he brought out the ball pen and made a show of several tries and failures at getting the point to stay out. Out of the corner of his eye he saw he had the three jurors farthest from Kane interested.

"Now, doctor, tell us about Miss Bailey's memory failure." Kane had Doc's eyes trapped in his glare; and Doc seemed to shrivel.

Holt unscrewed the sections of his ball point pen, and the spring inside flipped the cartridge of ink onto the floor in front of the lanky juror nearest the front of the courtroom. Retrieving it, Holt saw a fourth juror enjoying his efforts with the pen.

"Well," Doc evaded, "all of us get forgetful when we get older."

"Exactly!" Kane's voice cracked like a bull whip. He had the jurors again. "And that's because the blood doesn't get up into the brain like it used to, isn't it, doctor?"

"Well," Dr. Hardwick squirmed. "That happens, of course. But . . ."

"And the memory failure, the lack of orientation that results — that's called senile dementia, isn't it, Dr. Hardwick?"

"Are we talking about Adelaide Bailey?" Dr. Hardwick gained courage as he lost patience, and his voice sharpened. "These things are matters of degree. Adelaide's a long way from senile."

"Naturally, doctor," Kane observed kindly, "none of us wants to admit that old friends of our own generation have become senile."

Then, abruptly, he turned his back on the witness, walked over to the counsel table and lounged on the edge of it. When he addressed Doc again, his expression and tone had become supercilious.

"Are you a specialist in mental diseases, doctor?"

"No," Dr. Hardwick said stubbornly, "but I think I can tell if somebody's crazy."

"Have you done graduate work in mental diseases, doctor?"

"No, but . . ."

"Written any articles in the field?"

"No, but I tell you . . ."

"You're not a member of any organization of doctors specializing in psychiatry, are you?"

"I never applied, but I tell you . . ."

"So you don't claim to have the same qualifications to diagnose a case of senile dementia as such experts would," Kane concluded smoothly.

"Now just a minute," Doc protested. "I guess I can come about as close as a couple of geniuses who haven't even seen Adelaide."

Kane hesitated.

Holt smiled broadly, turning slightly in his chair so the jurors wouldn't miss this indication that Doc had scored on

15

Kane.

The big lawyer scowled. "The law allows hypothetical questions when it's necessary to get at the truth," he asserted hotly.

Holt started to his feet, but the judge waved him down. "The jury will ignore that," Judge Woodruff snapped. "Mr. Kane, stick to questions, please."

Kane dropped his manner of contemptuous indifference. He stalked back to the witness stand and stood over the doctor.

"Of course, you've never made a diagnosis without actually seeing the patient, have you?" he sneered.

Doc squirmed in his chair. "Well . . ."

"A bad night," Kane persisted. "A telephone call from a mother who told you the child's age, his temperature, described the round red spots on the skin."

"Well, naturally," Dr. Hardwick admitted, "you'd know —"

"Exactly! Just as Miss Bailey's advanced age, loss of memory, and erratic conduct spell senile dementia to a specialist without having to see her." Kane slammed the lid on that matter and walked back to the counsel table.

Turning, he resumed his attack. "Now, Doctor, I believe you were at a medical convention. Tell us, were you subpoenaed to come back here?"

Dr. Hardwick admitted no subpoena had forced his appearance in court.

"Then tell me, doctor, if you weren't subpoenaed," Kane gave a short laugh, "how much are you being paid to come down here and swear Adelaide Bailey is of sound mind?"

Holt felt a rush of heat in the back of his neck. Doc was too decent to be handled that way.

But this was no time to interfere, and Holt knew it. *Down, boy!* he warned himself. *Don't get your dander up!*

And don't help Kane emphasize his point by objecting to the question, either. The matter of fee was legitimate, even if the question had been put in objectionable form.

"Well, the question of a fee was never discussed." Dr. Hardwick seemed mildly surprised that anyone thought it should have been.

Holt made a mental note for redirect examination to show Doc never drove a bargain in advance of rendering medical service.

"So you're just down here to swear that Miss Bailey is sane, and you don't know how much you're going to get paid for this valuable service or even if you're going to get paid at all."

Doc nodded.

Kane sneered. "And that's as true as all the rest of your testimony."

Holt's patience snapped. "Your honor, I object . . . ."

"Sustained!" Judge Woodruff bit out the words.

Kane walked to his place at the counsel table and picked up one of the long ruled tablets that lawyers favor. Returning to the witness stand, he took a fountain pen from his pocket, leisurely unscrewed the cap and began to write.

For a full minute he stood there making notes. Like a scorekeeper impartially totaling the points to see who won the last rubber at bridge. Finally he smiled as though he had reached a pleasant conclusion.

"No further questions," he announced.

Holt reached for his own legal pad with his notes for redirect examination. Not focusing on it, he tried to appraise the effectiveness of Kane's stunt. Kane hadn't actually got Doc to change his testimony. But jurors often remembered the lawyer's leading questions as being the witness's answers.

And Kane's stage bit of adding up the score, smiling like he'd won, sure as hell might confuse the jury.

Now Kane came around the table. He still held his legal pad and fountain pen. Rather awkwardly he tried to hold the pad in one hand and still use that hand to screw the cap back on his pen.

As he passed Holt, he dropped pad, cap, and pen. The point of the pen stabbed into Holt's thigh, ink splattered his trousers, and the pen fell at his feet.

"Sorry. I'm terribly sorry." Kane pulled out a handkerchief and dabbed ineffectually at the spotted trousers.

Instinctively Holt leaned down to retrieve the objects on the floor. His fingers touched the pen. Simultaneously, Kane's heavy foot came down on Holt's open hand, though not with full weight. Holt winced, but the pain was bearable.

Kane bent down. His face almost touched Holt's. If he were aware his foot was on Holt's hand, he gave no sign of it.

Now Kane faced only Holt. Gone was the pleasant smile. Gone the polite mask. His eyes glittered; narrowed. He resembled nothing so much as a striking serpent. The foot on Holt's hand twisted as it crushed down with two hundred and twenty-five pounds of pressure. Holt went rigid with pain. Shock was so great that, for the instant, he couldn't even cry out.

Kane put his mouth to Holt's ear. So close Holt felt the hot spit of Kane's hiss. "Try your shyster tricks on me, will you!"

Sweeping up his tablet and pen then, Kane straightened and walked away.

Holt's paralysis broke. Fury swept through him. Exploding into action, he tore after Kane, swung him around, checked the impulse to strike, and instead grasped the lapels of Kane's frock coat.

"See here . . ." Holt started.

But Kane began to gasp for breath. Holt dropped his

hands and stepped back.

Kane tottered to an empty chair and sagged into it. Clutching his chest, he bent forward.

Holt swung round to call Doc from the witness stand. Dr. Hardwick was already hurrying toward Kane.

Straightening slightly, Kane fumbled in his coat pocket and brought out a small plastic container. Dr. Hardwick knelt, took the vial from Kane's hand and glanced at the label pasted to it.

Kneeling beside Dr. Hardwick, Holt watched anxiously. The doctor shook a pill out of the vial into his hand. The tiny white disk looked like the tablets Holt had seen Adelaide use.

"Nitroglycerin," Dr. Hardwick said. He put the pellet under Kane's tongue. "Did you know Kane had angina pectoris?"

Holt shook his head. "Will he be okay?" he demanded.

The doctor started to put his ear against Kane's chest. Kane pushed him away.

"Pain's almost gone," Kane panted.

Holt put his hand on Kane's arm. "Better let Doc check you," he said.

Kane pulled his arm away and continued to breathe heavily.

Dr. Hardwick stood up. "He'll be all right in a couple of minutes. Complexions too good for it to be a heart attack. These angina spells pass quickly . . . soon as the nitroglycerin dilates the blood vessels."

Relieved, Holt got to his feet and looked to see what effect the episode had had on the jury. The jurors' eyes were fixed on the slumped figure of Kane. Momentarily, the lanky one turned toward Holt and gave him a stoney stare. Holt winced.

Gradually Kane's breathing returned to normal. Judge Woodruff cleared his throat. Holt faced the bench.

Head cocked to his right, Judge Woodruff glared down through his awful, cadaverous left eye. Holt overcame his revulsion and forced himself to face the fierce, pallid stare.

"Court's adjourned until tomorrow morning," Judge Woodruff rasped. "Mr. Lawson, I want to see you in my chambers right now!"

Chapter 2

Numbly, Holt made his way back to the counsel table and sank into his chair.

He'd been had! Kane had purposely provoked him; and he had charged to take the bait.

His blood cooled; chilled. That look from the lanky juror told him that now they were against him, convinced Adelaide was crazy. Didn't her own doctor think so? No need for the jury to sift Doc's testimony, analyze it for themselves. Adelaide's own lawyer had saved them the trouble. He'd blown his stack when Kane made Doc back down on calling the old gal sane.

And it wouldn't help Holt's case that he'd attacked an older man . . . a man who'd repeatedly demonstrated his devoutness to the jury with Biblical quotations . . . a man with a heart condition.

Dr. Hardwick came and stood by the counsel table. His eyes looked past Holt toward the door out to the hall. But he turned back. "Do you want me again in the morning, Holt? I'm willing to give it another try if it'll help."

Holt smiled wryly. "Sorry, but what I need is a dependable, truthful witness . . . which, thanks to me, isn't your present reputation with that jury."

He turned to Burgess. Already on her feet, she chucked

notebooks and pencils into her purse and snapped it shut.

"Call Shelton and get him to be here first thing in the morning, will you?" Holt asked. "This chewing out may take some time."

"I hope it's long enough to do some good," Burgess replied, her voice sharp with exasperation. She started off.

"Burgess, —" Holt began. But the sound of impatient throat-clearing claimed his attention. Turning, he saw Woodruff waiting beside his elevated bench. Holt joined the judge and followed His Honor into his chambers.

Everything in Judge Woodruff's office was of huge proportions except the judge himself. Crossing to an oversized mahogany desk that dominated the center of the room, the jurist turned and with a quick gesture indicated the couch and chairs that crammed the office.

"Sit down," he ordered. Then, ignoring the high-backed swivel desk chair, he perched on the edge of the desk itself.

Holt chose the enormous leather couch where, by sitting on the edge, he could keep his feet under him. He had no desire to prolong the interview.

From his vantage point atop the desk, Judge Woodruff glared down through his ghastly whitish left eye. "Holt, what the hell am I going to do with you?" he rasped.

Holt made himself meet the distasteful stare. "Judge, I guess we'll have to condition my reflexes so I smile sweetly when a hulk like Kane stamps on my hand."

"So that was it." Judge Woodruff cocked his head to focus with his less virulent right eye, but his voice continued harsh. "I can nip that kind of contempt in the bud . . . given any kind of cooperation."

"I know. I know." Restive, Holt started to his feet, remembered his honor's dislike of the rest of mankind's towering over him, and squatted again on the edge of the couch. "Judge, I'm sorry. But, whatever it looked like, I didn't even touch Kane."

"What it looked like was that you went berserk when Kane cut your witness to pieces. And that attack he had really cooked your goose."

Holt found the couch increasingly uncomfortable. He shifted position. "It was the first I ever knew of his having a heart condition," he said.

"First time it ever happened in my court," the judge acquiesced. "I understand he won a murder case over at Tyler that way. Collapsed right after his final argument. Jury figured he'd given his all for an innocent client."

"Are you saying he fakes those attacks?" Holt pulled at his chin and tried to think how such information could be used.

"Of course I'm not," the judge snapped. "How would I know? It's not my concern. It *is* my concern that you created a disturbance in my court. And that your conduct . . . not Adelaide's . . . may cause that jury to bring in a verdict of insanity."

The couch became unbearable. Holt got to his feet and leaned over the back of the chair nearest him, keeping his head level with the judge's.

For a few moments Judge Woodruff studied his own reflection in the glass fronts of the book cases lining the walls. Finally he turned back, and his right eye lined up on Holt while the colorless left one stared into space. "You check in with the sheriff and spend a day in jail for contempt," he said without rancor. "That and Kane's attack give me grounds for declaring a mistrial. Adelaide will be entitled to a new trial with a new lawyer."

"A mistrial!" Holt straightened, careless of overtopping his honor. His body, conditioned to respond to crises with physical action, pumped adrenalin into his system. Unused

23

for battle, it played the devil with his insides. He struggled to calm down and consider matters logically.

Would Adelaide be ahead by starting over? Hell, no. The case could be won with Shelton's testimony. No more weeks of worry for Adelaide.

And certainly no more of his father's old clients were going to drift back to the re-opened law office if this runt branded Holt inept by declaring a mistrial.

Judge Woodruff seemed to read his mind. "Your father was my friend and a damned good lawyer, Holt. I think he'd agree with me. We've had a succession of incidents that show you've got too low a boiling point for a lawyer. Go back to professional football."

Holt started. "No!"

"Why? You were good at it."

"I'll never go back," Holt said flatly. He forced his mind to block out the memories that tried to flood in.

The judge peered through his friendly brown eye. "I'm not trying to hurt you, Holt," he said kindly. "I'm trying to do what's best for Adelaide . . . and for you. You may have been famous for getting on a rampage and tearing up the opponents' line; but, in the courtroom, Kane's bested you a couple of times by baiting you into blowing up."

Holt took a deep breath. Somehow he had to break through Woodruff's self-righteousness without arousing the little gamecock's combativeness.

"I know you're thinking of Dad and Adelaide and what's best for everyone," Holt said. "But if you declare a mistrial when Adelaide counts on the case being won with Shelton's testimony, she's going to figure you conspired with the others to put her away."

"Adelaide has been my friend for many years," the judge said carefully. "But I have to do what I consider right."

Holt nodded agreement. "Of course. But Adelaide's going to be around to even scores. I'll win this case with Shelton's testimony. Or the next lawyer will. And then . . . well, I don't want Adelaide feeling about you like she did about Judge Thorp."

Holding his breath then, he watched for Woodruff's reaction. Adelaide had ruined Judge Thorp. She'd taken it as a personal affront when Thorp awarded custody of Reg to his mother, a trollop who'd driven Adelaide's brother to suicide. The campaign she'd financed against Thorp had been so vicious the man had quit the district.

Judge Woodruff swung around on his desk and glared through his colorless left eye. "Are you threatening me?"

That was precisely what Holt was doing, and he knew it. But he answered meekly. "No. I'm just saying I don't want Pinewood to lose a good judge. The years haven't mellowed Adelaide any."

For a few moments Judge Woodruff pinched and kneaded his upper lip between thumb and forefinger. Then, abruptly he pushed off the desk and stood facing Holt.

"Pay the clerk a ten dollar fine," he ordered.

No mistrial! Holt could go on with the case and win it. He sucked in a deep, happy breath.

But then Judge Woodruff pointed his right forefinger and sighted down it with a gruesome, angry eye. Holt checked an impulse to back away from the unlovely figure.

"You just bullied me into your last reprieve, Holt," the judge declared, his voice harsh with resentment. "The next time you get out of line, you won't practice another day in my court, or in any other court if I can help it!"

Holt stepped out of Judge Woodruff's office, shoved the door closed as quickly as he could without slamming it, and drew a big breath. These days it seemed the only pleasure he got from a chat with the judge was in reaching its end.

The clock that hung on the rear wall facing the judge's bench said five thirty. Connie would be dropping by the house shortly for a before-dinner drink.

The thought cheered Holt.

But Connie also would pepper him with questions about the trial, and that was a different matter — one that made him turn his thoughts to whether there might be any messages at the office.

The courtroom seemed forsaken. A drained pitcher stood near the witness chair and a gavel lay on the judge's desk, like props on a bare stage. Rows of empty seats awaited the spectators who would come to see the adversaries square off.

Deserted now by actors and audience alike, the room lay silent, hushed as an empty theater.

Holt circled the judge's bench.

Beyond it, Burgess sat waiting in the same chair she had used that afternoon. Crossing to her, Holt eased himself down on the edge of the table beside her. Her coat was still off, and his vantage point gave him a titillating sight of the start of the cleft and swell of two firm, tanned breasts.

"No phone calls," Burgess said. "I locked up and came over to see if I still had a job."

Holt grinned, still feeling his relief. "I won't fire you for a moment's cheekiness."

"Hmmph!" Burgess scoffed. "My worry was that you might have been put away as an habitual offender — Holt, how an intelligent man can fly into a tantrum like an unspanked child . . ." Burgess's flimsy blouse began to rise and fall with short, quick breaths.

"You look like a feisty kitten," Holt said. He took her by the arms, lifted her to her feet. "Relax. We got off with a fine and tomorrow we're going to break out of our losing streak."

"Woodruff must be going soft," Burgess snapped. But her

eyes showed her relief, and she stepped forward and gave him a quick, slight hug.

Then she pulled back. But the momentary pressure of her body and the mixed smell of delicate scent and animal odor intrigued Holt.

He took a firmer grip on her arms. Burgess strained away from him.

For a moment he held her locked against him. Then Burgess let herself go limp. Holt could have sworn her temperature dropped fifteen degrees. The body he was clasping to him had the feel of a dead dolphin.

He dropped his arms and pretended to shiver. "Br-r-r! for a second there I thought blood ran in your veins."

"I thought everybody knew better than that," Burgess snatched up her purse and coat. "But if it did, you wouldn't be the man to warm it."

"Meaning you don't like the athletic anthropoid type?" Holt teased.

Burgess started for the door, then paused.

"Meaning," she corrected, "that I haven't the slightest desire to play stand-in for your dear little Connie!"

Chapter 3

Thoroughly peeved with himself, Holt stamped across the courthouse lawn to his car. Giving in to the sudden impulse to hug Burgess had been a piece of asininity. They had a good, friendly, professional relationship. And anyway, everybody knew she tolerated men only so long as they kept their maleness in check.

The door of the station wagon stuck. Holt wrenched it open, glad of something to vent his irritation on. It nettled him to have both judge and Burgess treat him like a bad-tempered adolescent. All the more so because they were right. He *had* discredited Doc's testimony — testimony that would have weighed heavily with the jury — by blowing up.

Uncomfortably aware that he was singing a too-familiar refrain, Holt promised himself that from this moment he'd keep his natural instincts on the bench and let the old intellect call the signals.

One of the new air-conditioned coaches at the side of Lone Star Drug and Bus Depot had half of Elm Street blocked. Detouring around it, Holt drove rapidly out the wide, tree-lined avenue.

Here and there neighbors were working in the flower gardens that dotted large, well-tended lawns. Holt observed small town courtesy and returned their waves without really thinking about it. He was busy trying to cheer himself with the prospect of before-dinner drinks with Connie.

The two-story white frame that had been his parents' home came into view. At the approach of the car, Snubby awakened from his nap in the front porch swing, cocked his head and plunged down the porch steps. Amused, Holt drove to the back yard and called a needless, "Here Snubby!" as he got out of the Chevy.

Already under foot, the pug-nosed little Pekingnese danced around on short, sturdy hind legs.

Holt reached down to fluff Snubby's long brown hair, then scooped the tiny dog into his arms. "Lonesome, weren't you? I'm surprised you didn't go find some mischief."

Snubby wriggled to get closer, his tongue busy as an aspen leaf in a breeze. Once or twice Holt hoisted him and let him get in a few licks on the cheek.

Gradually Snubby subsided. Pulling gently on the little fellow's ears, Holt scratched at the sensitive spots behind them.

Blood appeared on his fingers. "Darn you, Snubby," Holt grumbled. "You've been picking on some Great Dane again."

Snubby started trying to wriggle free. But Holt carried him into the house, plopped him in the kitchen sink and washed the wound clean.

A search of the kitchen cabinets revealed no household antiseptic. Holt hauled down a bottle of Scotch whiskey and doused the wound with that.

Snubby let out a yelp of indignant surprise and made a prodigious leap out of the sink, over the drain board, and down to the floor.

Unthinkingly, Holt laughed. At the sound, Snubby got a hurt look on his face and slunked out of the room.

"Come here, boy," Holt called. But Snubby didn't reappear.

Holt sighed. Laughter equalled ridicule where Snubby was concerned. No use putting food down until they made up.

Fixing a drink with the Scotch he'd used on Snubby, he went into the living room.

Snubby sulked on the divan.

"Hey, boy, I wasn't laughing at you." Holt sat down beside the furry little pooch. "I was proud of you. Snubby's a good boy."

Snubby lay motionless.

Holt continued the gentle, meaningless murmur, occasionally interrupting it to sip at his drink, while with the fingers of his free hand he scratched Snubby on top of the head.

After a while a warm tongue brushed Holt's hand in forgiveness.

Relaxed by the drink and the process of soothing Snubby, Holt stretched into an almost horizontal position on the couch. Soon, however, the low familiar purr of Connie's car moved past the living room windows.

Holt snapped out of his lassitude and hurried to the back door. Connie's snappy-looking sports job stood beside his station wagon like a fine-limbed Arabian next to a draft horse.

Connie ran up the back stairs, the swirl of her skirt revealing slender brown legs. Holt pushed the screen door open, put his hands around her waist and lifted her with ease a foot off the ground so her eyes came level with his.

She took his face in her small hands and kissed him. A heady perfume quickened his pulse. He squeezed her tighter.

"Put me down, you monster," Connie gasped.

Holt lowered her to the floor. Connie pulled off her bandeau. The sheen of her chestnut hair caught up little flecks of green in her hazel eyes. Her radiance dissolved the

31

last of the irritation and strain he had brought from the courtroom.

A growl sounded from the kitchen door . . . grew in intensity.

"Oh, oh. Snubby smells Ming on me," Connie said.

"Well, he can go find somebody else's cat to tangle with." Holt picked Snubby up, shoved him through the small hole with the canvas flap and blocked the entrance with a box. "You'd think he'd learn that growling at you rates a one-way ticket out."

"Don't worry, he will," Connie asserted. Then her tone became gay. "Have you hauled down the cocktail pennant?"

"The flag flies high." Holt got busy bringing together Scotch, ice, and soda.

They took their drinks into the living room. Connie brushed the worst of the dog hairs from the divan and piled pillows against the wall. Circling the room, Holt pulled the blinds shut and achieved a semidarkness that obscured the dust and drabness of his bachelor's quarters.

When she had made a back of the pillows, Connie stretched out against them, her legs in front of her. Her skirt tightened, outlining a figure that managed to be at once slender yet provocatively full.

Holt felt a magnetic pull. He crossed to her. Connie moved over and patted the spot beside her invitingly. Somehow she managed to make the small gesture exciting.

Accepting the invitation, Holt joined her on the couch and began to hurry his drink, relishing the warmth the liquor and Connie's nearness sent running through his body.

Connie emptied her glass, then turned and smiled lazily. Small, even teeth harmonized with her delicately pretty features while, in contrast, a more generously proportioned mouth promised a taste for earthy enjoyment.

Holt gulped the last of his drink, reached for her and

32

kissed the soft hollow between her neck and shoulder. Connie drew back to face him, lips parted. But for the moment he tantalized himself by kissing the lids of her eyes.

Suddenly Connie reached up, pulled his head down and gave him a hard kiss. Then she drew back, laughed, and got to her feet.

Her withdrawal intensified the need of her that had started in Holt. He started after her.

"Not so fast! You take me home again looking like we've been on a bivouac, and Dad will get his shotgun down." Connie worked with the buttons of her blouse. "This time I'm prepared."

The blouse came off. Bare shoulders glistened in the semidarkness. Conscious of a warmth beginning to run through his veins, Holt pushed up to a sitting position.

Connie whipped off her shirt . . . stood there in a fairly decorous play suit.

Tanned flesh gleamed in the half light, revealing a slender waist and well-proportioned, surprisingly sturdy thighs. Coming up off the couch fast, Holt clutched the soft, naked middle.

Connie shrieked, then threw her bare arms around him.

His shirt destroyed her closeness. He ripped it off. Connie's hands caressed his naked back.

It wasn't enough. He wanted her nakedness all up against his nakedness.

Her bra proved to be a stretch affair. He pulled it over her head and free of her arms. Connie's breasts, young, firm and swollen hard, throbbed against his bare chest.

He strained all of her against him, passionately, pressing the warm female flesh against his body. Connie lifted her head and opened wide her mouth. Holt kissed her. Full lips molded themselves to his — following, responding.

Then all at once she darted her tongue into his mouth, a

sudden thrust of passion. Her body seemed to abandon its independence and interlock with his. He caught hold of her well-formed hips, one in each hand, and pressed them in toward his thighs in a frenzy of need for consummation and relief.

Connie's body thrust against him.

Sweeping her up, Holt stretched her on the couch and fumbled at her shorts — flipping the buttons open, yanking at the zipper tab, pulling the playsuit to her knees.

But Connie's vital areas, it now developed, lay sheathed in a girdle. The tight fitting elastic fabric presented an impregnable defense line that wouldn't admit even a finger.

Frustrated, incredulous, he pulled back, breathing heavily. "Not that damned girdle again! Not with a play suit!"

Connie leaned across him, put her generous mouth on his, and pressed her body against him with an intensifying, demanding rhythm.

Angrily, he shoved her back. "Connie, we're too old for that kind of juvenile squirming."

Connie voice was small. "I don't want you going to one of your Tyler trollops."

The vital energy that had generated itself in him, unexpended, racked him like a motor racing in a parked car. He laughed shortly. "You think twitching against that girdle's a substitute?"

Connie let out a sound somewhere between a sob and a moan. He sensed a shudder go through her. Then she drew in a deep sigh. "Holt, in about five minutes of clumsy, graceless wriggling I can get out of this chastity belt. If you want me to, I will . . ."

He kissed her — a perfunctory, loveless gesture. "For God's sake, Connie, start wriggling!"

"I mean, if you want it that much, I will. But if I do, I

34

won't marry you."

Holt stifled an impatient snort. He reached for his shirt and tossed Connie her halter.

"Okay," he said. "You know I'm not going to say that I don't want anything more from you than a quick lay."

Shaking, Connie drew the halter across her breasts. "Try to understand, Holt. You've been through one broken marriage. I don't want you seeing Trix when you look at me."

Holt thrust his arms into the sleeves of his shirt and attacked the matter of buttoning it. "Stop talking about Trix. She hasn't got anything to do with us."

"Oh yes she has. When we're married, I don't want you looking at me across the breakfast table and wondering how I'll spend the day."

He felt his temperature rise. "Hell, Connie, you're nothing like that bitch."

"Right. But deep down, she left you with doubts about all women. So I'm going to demonstrate control when you've got me so wound up I can hardly stand it. When we're married, there'll be plenty of times you'll be glad to remember that I can . . . and that marriage means something to me."

Holt shrugged. "Okay, Connie, if that's the way you feel. But let's skip the frills and get married."

"That suits me." Connie tugged her shorts back up around her waist. "When the trial's over?"

Holt nodded. "When this trial's over. Then I'll know I have Adelaide's business sewed up. And Dad's old clients will drift back once I show I can handle Kane."

Connie sat straight up. "You're that sure of the case, Holt?"

"It'll be all right." Holt made his voice confident. "Even though I messed up Doc's testimony today. I . . ."

"I was there," Connie interrupted.

Holt cocked an eyebrow.

"All right, I know," Connie sounded like a little girl admitting to being naughty. "But I can't bother you when you don't know I'm there."

Holt shrugged. Then he stood, pushed his shirt tail into his trousers and began to pace as though he were already in the courtroom. "It won't matter about Doc. Just get the idea over to the jury that Reg is grabbing for control of Adelaide's money, and they won't give a damn what the doctors said."

Connie leaned on crossed knees, an intent expression on her face. "I want to talk to you about that, Holt," she said.

Holt stopped pacing. "About what?"

"About having Shelton testify to Reggie's debts . . . what that gambler threatens if Reggie doesn't pay . . . all that."

"Connie, I can't help it if Reg has been close to your family. It's the only way to win the case."

"Reg has been talking to Dad. He says if you don't make a fool of him in public, he'll let Dad keep you on as the bank's lawyer."

Holt snorted. "That's a trick of Kane's. He knows that would cinch a win for him."

"But still, Reg would do what he promised Dad." Connie left the couch and came to stand near Holt. "Even if you win, Adelaide can't live much longer."

"Don't worry. I haven't forgotten about number one. Adelaide's business will be run by the bank as trustee. That means your father. Reg won't have a damn thing to do with it except cash his check every month and live it up."

"That's the other thing I want to tell you. Reg told Dad there isn't any will. He says he'll inherit Adelaide's estate outright."

The opposition was running the plays so fast, Holt felt the need for a time out to analyze them. Frowning, he thrust his hands in his trouser's pockets and began to pace again. "So that's why your father ducked out on testifying. Reg would be his boss."

Connie moved into his path. "Holt, you said yourself we've got to have some income to get married on. All you have to do is leave Reg alone."

Her words started a burn under Holt's collar. "No dice," he snapped. "If I didn't show what's behind Reg's bringing this suit, I'd be throwing the game."

"It's your decision, Holt. It just seemed we could be sure the other way."

Retrieving her skirt and blouse as she spoke, Connie picked up the empty glasses, and sauntered into the kitchen. Holt followed, making a conscious effort to calm down. Carefully he went over what she'd said — trying to figure the angles, fix the odds. One detail troubled him.

"Connie," he said, "I think your father better come down tomorrow and let me put him on the stand. Just to say Adelaide's sane. I won't ask him about Reg; Shelton's promised to testify on that. But Adelaide's already writing names in her black book."

Connie plunked down the things she was carrying and put her hands on Holt's arm. Her brow furrowed with concern. "Dad can't take that chance, Holt. He's getting old. You know how much he lost in the market. Don't ask him to fall out with Reg."

Holt pictured Adelaide shaking her cane and ordering him to arrange Townsend's firing.

"Connie," he insisted, "Shelton's testimony is going to blow Reggie's case out of the water. And then Adelaide's going to gut every poor devil who hasn't stuck by her."

The little hands on his arms tightened desperately. Connie pled with her eyes. "You'll have to stop her, Holt. You can. You'll be her fair-haired boy if you win this case.

She'll take an excuse from you for Dad's not testifying."

Holt put his arms around her. "Maybe. I don't know. Your dad's taking an awful chance."

Connie gave him a quick kiss. Then she held tight to him. "Not as big a chance as you're taking, Holt. Either way, there's hope for Dad. But you're gambling every plan we've made on winning that case tomorrow!"

Long after Connie had left, Holt paced the kitchen floor, ticking off in his mind questions for Shelton, points to cover in his argument to the jury, and how to handle Adelaide after the case was closed.

One thing for sure, he'd have to find out if Adelaide had played around with her will and fouled it up. Reggie's crack about inheriting outright sounded as though she might. And however much Adelaide might dote on her no-good nephew, she wouldn't want her enterprises going to pot under his bungling.

For his own part, the very thought of Reg in control made his head ache. He wished he weren't so wide awake. It might have been better if he hadn't shunned Connie's half-way measures.

Trouble was, he simply couldn't buy her logic, let alone that damned nonsense with the girdle. His misery with Trix didn't warrant such.

It seemed, however, that he hadn't too much choice about Connie's reactions.

He sucked in a breath and exhaled vigorously. Bad luck from Trix was nothing new. Except for her, he'd still be playing the game he loved at a salary he loved. But could Connie be right about what Trix had done to him?

He hadn't been suspicious of Trix. Disappointed, of course, when he found her frigid. But a contract was a contract, and she could put on a great act up to a point.

Besides, who'd have suspected that a frigid woman would make like a nymphomaniac? Certainly he hadn't. Not until the snickering in the locker room got so loud that he realized that in their own dumb way the guys were trying to tell him something.

Even then he'd had to check it out to believe it.

Coming back to the present, Holt mixed himself a dark brown drink and leaned against the drainboard. And even as he drank, he knew he was doing it in order to deaden the hurt that always came. He had no desire to relive the night the phone call had come, the dash for his car, the long agonizing ride. But he knew that he would . . .

The team had been on the road a couple of weeks, and he hadn't even known that Trix had followed them. At the edge of town, his headlights had picked up the notice, "Dallas City Limit", then the luminous signs that showed the night speed limits and obscured those for daytime. Thirty-five. Forty-five. Fifty-five.

At last the dazzling neon sign, "Paradise Motel". The nondescript sedan parked near the outdoor phone booth.

A slender young man in horn-rimmed glasses slipped from the sedan's front seat and came over. "I'm from the agency. They're in cabin 48. I got a key."

Cabins, strung in the usual quadrangle around the usual swimming pool. With an effort, Holt forced the shaking-stiff tension from his muscles and got out of the car.

"Who's the guy?" he demanded.

The young man reached into his sedan and produced a camera with flash bulb attachment that he strung around his neck. "I don't know his name. He's a big, red faced, potbellied fellow. He was out at the stadium with the team."

"That's Blake." Holt clenched his fists. "I knew the front office figured it owned *my* body. Looks like . . ."

"Got a gun?" the young man interrupted.

39

"Why, no. I . . ."

"Good." The detective looked down at Holt's big hands balled into fists. "But I'm still not going in if there's going to be rough stuff. I've got my license to think about."

Holt unclenched his fists. "I'm okay," he promised. "I'll be satisfied to be rid of the bitch."

The young man held out a key. Holt took tight hold of it. Together they made their way around the courtyard to the cabin marked 48. The bookish young man lifted his camera in both hands and nodded.

Holt twisted the key and shoved open the door simultaneously; flicked on the lights and swiveled aside.

Beside him a flash bulb exploded. Blinking his eyes back into focus, he saw Trix clutching a sheet up around herself and her bed mate. Only her pale startled face and Blake's round, ruddy features were visible.

Striding to the bed, Holt snatched the sheet out of her hands.

The flash bulb exploded again. Trix tried unsuccessfully to hide her lovely naked curves behind Blake's great beer belly.

Finally Blake managed to suck in some air. His gray eyes recaptured some of their chill air of command. "Holt," he said flatly, "I'll blacklist you with every pro team in the country."

"You scare hell out of me." Holt let his body relax against the closet door. "Where I'm going, they've barely heard of pro football."

And to Trix: "Baby, when I send you the divorce papers, you get them back signed by return mail."

He'd gone out, then, and shut the door with a decisive snap that had closed Trix out of his life.

So now, here he was back in Pinewood and about to stick his foot into the tender trap again. The tender trap . . . Surprised, Holt took another drink and ran that last sentiment by for a closer look. A hell of a way to put into words the marrying of a girl like Connie.

So Connie was right. He was still bitter, and wary along with it. And now he knew that what with the lawsuit and Connie and Trix chasing themselves around in his mind, he wasn't likely to get the rest he needed for tomorrow's trial.

He reached for the bottle of Scotch and slugged his drink with enough to insure himself a rest of sorts for at least a few hours and marched upstairs to bed.

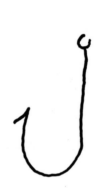

Chapter 4

The Scotch slugged Holt into instant sleep. But in a couple of hours the alcohol had overheated him. He woke, his body drenched with sweat, the smell of stale liquor in his nostrils.

Toward dawn he dropped off again into troubled dreams: The opposition team was tough. The muddy field sucked at his feet. But it didn't seem to bother Shelton. Ball in hand, he danced around Holt like Peter Pan tantalizing Goliath.

Holt grabbed and fell. The mud held him helpless.

Now Kane appeared, driving a mowing machine. A warning bell, like an ice cream vendor's, kept sounding; but Holt struggled in vain to free himself from the muck. The slashing blades bore down on him. Kane leered evilly. Br-i-i-ing! Bri-i-i-ing! The continued jangle of the warning bell in Holt's ear set his teeth on edge.

With a desperate effort, he pulled himself free of the slush and rolled upright, all at once awake and back in his own room again.

The telephone on his night stand let out one more jarring "bri-i-ing". Holt grabbed for it.

Miss Phoebe had the chipper sound of one who'd been up for hours. "You need something warm in your stomach today," she said. "Come up and I'll give you a real breakfast."

Holt waited until he'd shaken Kane and Shelton and the mowing machine out of his mind. No doubt Adelaide had a full report on yesterday's fiasco and was ready to raise hell.

"Sorry," he regretted. "I've got a lot of things . . ."

Miss Phoebe broke in: "Adelaide says to come."

Holt put his hand over the mouthpiece and breathed a "damn!". Then he spoke into the phone. "Okay. Be there quick as I douse myself awake."

He shaved quickly, then made adjustments to the shower's nozzle head and turned the cold water on full. A stinging, chilling spray shot out. It cleared his head and put the snap back in his body. Dressing, he headed his station wagon out Elm Street.

A couple of blocks past Burgess' house, Elm came to a dead end at the grounds of the Townsend and Bailey estates. Holt paused before turning into Adelaide's driveway and looked on ahead to where the Townsends' English manor house loomed atop a terraced hill.

Already Connie had the french doors of her bedroom thrown open to the sun. Holt smiled and moved on. It looked as though she planned to ignore his ban again and slip into the courtroom.

Adelaide's white-columned mansion, set well back from the street, looked like some official government residency. Holt stopped smiling. Jaw set, he drove up the curving roadway toward a meeting with his capricious client.

In spots a stubble of grass had taken over the graveled drive, Patches of paint had flaked off the tall, handsome columns. It gave the imposing mansion an air of decay.

The obvious deterioration bothered Holt. Frowning, he rang the bell and peeked through the window of the door while he waited.

44

Miss Phoebe, small and plump, shuffled down the hall and opened the front door. Holt stooped for a quick hug and kissed the round cheek she tilted up.

"Adelaide's waiting for you in the living room," Miss Phoebe said. "I'll bring your breakfast there."

Holt followed her down the tiled entrance hall. High ceilings, thick walls, and a profusion of ferns produced a quiet coolness in the house. But then Holt saw Miss Phoebe labor with all her might to get through the swinging door at the hall's end.

At that evidence of her failing strength, the quiet coolness changed to a deathly cold. Holt felt as though he were walking through a funeral parlor, and suddenly he ached for the bygone days when this house had been so lived-in, with a bustling Miss Phoebe to whip up cookies for the neighborhood children and an energetic Adelaide to boss their games, making sure nephew Reggie got his full turns at everything.

End of the hall. Holt entered the huge sunken living room. A gaunt, raw-boned caricature of her former self, Adelaide Bailey huddled by the far windows in a huge linen-covered chair, a shawl around her shoulders. Forgetting he'd been reluctant to come, Holt hurried to her.

The thick arms of the chair emphasized the wasting of Adelaide's large frame. But her black eyes had lost none of their piercing quality.

Holt stretched out his hand. Adelaide took it in a scrawny grasp that she suddenly strengthened, her mouth set with the effort.

"Your grip feels good and strong," Holt hastened to assure her.

Adelaide pointed to the sofa with a gnarled cane that she then laid across the arms of her chair. "Sit down, boy," she said.

Holt let himself onto the overstuffed couch, glad of the crisp white linen cover over the blue plush.

"I wondered how the case is going," Adelaide prompted. "You didn't call me last night."

Holt took a moment to study Adelaide, to take stock of the repelling fierceness of the powerful nose and chin in her gaunt face. Not until he was sure he'd recovered from any momentary mawkishness did he respond.

"We haven't time for you to play cat and mouse with me," he said firmly. "You've heard it from your pipe line. Yes, I suckered for one of Kane's tricks."

"I'm going to ruin Kane," she declared. Holt looked up, surprised at the complete absence of emotion in her voice. She'd uttered a straightforward statement of fact in the same tone she'd announce a decision to her board of directors. Seeing the cruel, hawk-like set of her mouth, Holt almost felt sorry for the old shyster.

Adelaide fingered her cane. "Bad news doesn't upset me as much as not being told. Reason I got you over here, I'm putting a stop to Doc and you deciding what I'm to hear and what I'm to do."

So she hadn't called him over to fire him. Holt relaxed against the back of the sofa.

Then shuffling steps sounded in the hall, and Miss Phoebe came in with a loaded tray. Holt hurried to take it from her. The mixed aroma of sausages, omelet, and freshly brewed coffee delighted his nostrils and griped his stomach with sudden hunger.

Apparently Miss Phoebe had her instructions from Adelaide. She made a quick exit. Holt glanced across the room. Adelaide had closed her eyes and rested her head against the back of her chair.

Happily undisturbed, Holt disposed of the solid food and began to sip his coffee.

46

Adelaide still had her eyes closed.

Holt looked at his wrist watch. "Adelaide," he said softly.

She showed no sign of hearing. He reminded himself that nowadays Adelaide simply tired in the middle of events which in the past would have kept her fired up.

He called a little louder, "Adelaide!"

The eyes opened then, although Adelaide let her head continue to rest against the chair. "Reginald's weak like his father was," she explained. "He begged me for money to settle his gambling debts before he brought this suit. He owes a man named Fox. Reginald says the fellow's going to kill him unless he pays off."

As Holt counted it, they'd discussed Reg's debts and Fox's threats a dozen times. More and more Adelaide repeated things. His coffee lost its rich flavor, and he put the cup on the tray and pushed it from him.

Adelaide seemed to be talking to herself more than to him. "I gave Reginald that dab of stock so's he'd take an interest in the bakery. Now he wants to take over and sell everything so he can get his money out of it."

If Adelaide had forgotten their previous conversations, Holt saw no reason not to try again for the easy out. "Buy his stock yourself, Adelaide," Holt urged. "Then Reg can pay off Fox. You'll be through with Reg's owning any part of the bakery."

Instantly, Adelaide stiffened. Sitting bolt upright, she leaned toward him across the cane that rested on the arms of her chair. "Boy, are you going soft? I've told you a dozen times I won't be blackmailed. No! No! No!"

"And I've told you a dozen times, 'Yes!' Ever since Doc said you weren't to come to court."

Adelaide brushed the idea aside with a wave of her cane and again let her head rest against the chair back. "You still

47

figure you can win with Shelton's testimony?" she demanded.

Holt nodded. "Once he tells that jury Reg would sell the plant to square a flock of debts, that'll end it. Those jurors aren't going to take any chances on Pinewood County's losing its big payroll."

"You can count on Shelton," Adelaide asserted. "I got him over here and put the fear of God into him."

Holt grimaced. "You shouldn't have. I had Sam all primed to go. He doesn't like being browbeaten."

Adelaide leaned across her cane, her fleshless face seamed with lines of cruelty. "I made him and I can break him and he might as well know it."

Now more than ever Holt wanted to talk to Shelton before court opened. He glanced at his watch and started to rise. Adelaide waved her cane.

"You just sit there," she ordered. "I haven't said what I sent for you to hear."

Holt settled on the edge of the couch. Impatient though he was, it raised his spirits to see Adelaide her old peppery self.

She gripped her cane in her fist. "The minute Shelton gets off that stand, you shoot Burgess to the nearest phone. If she can tell me the case is won, okay. But I want your solemn word on it."

Holt considered, then nodded soberly. "I've always leveled with you."

"If you can't, ..." she began.

"If I can't," Holt interrupted, "I'm going to take Kane and Reg aside and settle as best I can. Doc says . . ."

Adelaide's eyes flashed. "Alexander Hardwick nor anybody else tells me what I can do!"

She pushed herself to her feet as she spoke and stood before Holt, her cane held out like a staff of authority.

Straight-backed, she looked down at him like a queen, expecting — demanding — the fealty that was her due.

"Now you listen good, boy," she ordered. "There's lots of things worse than dying. If you can't tell me that case is won, the only other thing I want to hear out of Burgess is:

'Adelaide, Holt says for you to come arunning!' "

Chapter 5

A sadness came over Holt as he closed the door of Adelaide's house and walked toward his car. Her failing strength depressed him the more because strength had been the essence of Adelaide's being. And a sense of deep personal loss intensified his grief, for that strength had supported him at his mother's death, during his father's invalidism, and in all the other tight spots he'd gotten himself into, right down to the present one.

The day turned dark under the impact of his mood. Suddenly impatient, he spun the car's wheels on the gravel and headed for the courthouse.

On either side of Elm Street stood the substantial, well-maintained homes of merchants and professional men who made their living in Pinewood County. Now Holt took special note of these neat dwellings. For within a hundred miles, in other towns, ran a dozen similar streets lined with unpainted, decaying houses.

Not that Pinewood farmers had done any better in cotton than anyone else, but Adelaide's bank had lent them the money to shift to other crops and to livestock raising. And when the call for farm labor dried up because machines came in to plow, plant, pick, and pack, Adelaide's Breads, Inc., was mushrooming and screaming for more help.

But now the decay would start here, too, unless Holt could spike Reg's plan for the sale and roll-up of the baking plant.

Nervously, hardly aware of doing so, Holt picked up a sponge rubber ball from the dashboard. Forefinger straight, he crushed the ball in his left hand between the thumb and fingers that controlled his golf swing.

The ball was still in his hand, he discovered, when he parked at the courthouse square. Disgustedly, he heaved it into the back of the station wagon. He didn't need more muscle. He needed to learn to relax and swing that golf club easy. But he'd just exhibited the intensity that caused him to jump at the ball, top it and wind up on the fairway fifty yards behind some hundred-and-ten-pounder.

Inside the courthouse, as he entered, the single elevator had just started clanking its way upward. The clock on the wall said five minutes of nine. Holt took a couple of restless turns.

The ancient cage continued its slow journey. Unable to stand waiting longer, Holt sprinted up the stairs that wound around the elevator shaft. He knew himself too well to think he could relax until he'd reassured himself that his prime witness was still ready to go.

On the third floor the silhouettes of three men showed against the glare from the window at the end of the corridor. Holt identified Sam Shelton at once by the outline of his ankle-length trousers and narrow shouldered coat.

A large, solid figure loomed beside Shelton. Squinting against the light, Holt made out Kane's wavy gray hair and, at Kane's shoulder, Reg's shock of red curls.

What was Shelton doing fraternizing with the opposition? Frowning, Holt hurried toward the group.

Kane glanced up, pivoted and strode off toward the courtroom. Reg trotted at his heels.

Coming up to Shelton, Holt wiped the frown from his face and put out his hand. "Did you learn anything in the enemy's camp?" He tried to sound like he was joking.

At the same time he gave his witness a quick once-over. A jury of farmers weren't going to go for those carefully manicured nails and sartorial perfection. But Shelton did have his hair in a masculine, almost military clip. Above all, that open Nordic face bespoke honesty.

Shelton shook hands cordially enough. "Nobody's my enemy, Holt," he replied. "Not in a family squabble."

Holt stiffened. "Now wait a minute. This thing's more than that. There're a hell of a lot of jobs at stake."

"Including mine, apparently," Shelton scowled. "Adelaide acts like I couldn't get another spot. I could go to Dallas tomorrow. And my family wants to."

Groaning inwardly, Holt put his arm around Shelton's shoulder. "Sam, I know Adelaide raised hell with you," he soothed. "We all take some of it. But you're sticking by what you told me, aren't you?"

Just then Mr. Meade, the bailiff, appeared at the courtroom door and gestured. Holt nodded and, his arm still resting casually on Shelton's shoulder, started toward the clerk's entrance. But he strained his ear for Shelton's reply and readied himself to spin the smaller man around and have a showdown if there was any wavering.

"You'll get it word for word the way I've told it to you," Shelton answered. "She couldn't make me lie if she fired me."

Holt would have liked to get that commitment nailed down tighter. But the bailiff was waving again, most anxiously. For a second Holt hesitated. Then he gave Shelton a pat on the shoulder, dropped his arm and led the way through the clerk's office into the courtroom.

The clock on the rear wall showed it was only a few

seconds past nine o'clock. Judge Woodruff barely scowled and through his good eye at that.

Holt gestured Shelton to the witness stand and made his way to the counsel table. Burgess had grabbed their favorite side nearest the jury box where, as she put it, Holt could "force his personality out between his teeth" at the jurors.

But this morning Holt contented himself with displaying a sober mien. He had a feeling he might as well postpone wooing the jury with smiles until he regained some of the ground he'd lost the day before.

Anyway, none of the jurors seemed to be aware of his approach. Their eyes were otherwise occupied. He followed their stares.

Burgess had her stenographer's notebook open on her lap and her legs crossed to raise it to a handy level for writing. Her position had lifted and stretched her skirt so that, waist to ankle, such of her shapely curves as weren't exposed were amply delineated.

Flicking one of the heavy chairs around, Holt sat down beside her. "How about waiting until I've finished with the witness to take those jurors' minds to bed with you?" he suggested.

Burgess looked up at him, then down at the skirt. Without a word, she slapped her notebook on the big table and swung her legs beneath it.

Holt nodded approvingly. "You've got a better gimmick there than my trick pen. I'll give you the signal when to blitz Kane's cross examination."

Burgess directed her look to the front of the courtroom. "Shelton's being sworn," she observed. "You'd better get your mind out of the gutter long enough to question him."

Holt turned quickly to the front of the courtroom. Just lowering his right hand, Shelton looked down expectantly from the witness box. Judge Woodruff nodded briefly.

54

Holt glanced at his jury of farmers and back. Given his druthers, he'd shuck his main witness out of that hand-tailored suit and collar-ad shirt. But Shelton prided himself on not having gone native. Shrugging, Holt put his opening question: "Please state your name."

"Samuel B. Shelton."

"You've lived in Pinewood for a number of years?"

"I have."

"Mr. Shelton, will you please tell us the circumstances of your coming to Pinewood?"

Shelton explained that he'd come to Pinewood to work for Adelaide's Breads, Inc. as a junior executive. Holt's questioning brought out that he had actually been employed by Adelaide Bailey, then president of the corporation. Under Adelaide's presidency, the corporation had been financially successful, dominating the East Texas market for bread products of all kinds. Grooming Shelton, she had moved him from one executive position to another.

Holt got up. The stuffiness and warmth from many bodies would have his recently fed jury drowsy. Even the drone of the air conditioner, as it fought back against the heat, was calculated to lull them to sleep.

Walking the length of the jury box, he let his hand slide along the rail, feeling that special kind of smoothness that machining and planing and sanding can't give. The smoothness of generations of wear. Of jurors hanging on to let themselves down and haul themselves up. Of janitors oiling and rubbing and oiling again. And most of all of lawyers: lawyers slapping their palms on the rail for emphasis, pounding their fists against it in anger.

Continuing past the box, Holt stopped at the heavy bar separating the spectators from the business end of the courtroom.

The bar, the jury rail, judge's bench, and witness

55

stand — all had been hewn on massive proportions out of native oak. That heavy, close-grained hardwood had been there before any of those present. It would remain when every one on hand was gone. Just like the whole system of laws and judges and juries, hammered out from time immemorial and to be handed down for generations unforeseeable.

Mistakes there would always be, for men administered the system. But few they must be or the system would not be so durable.

The thought strengthened Holt's confidence. He turned back toward the witness stand and raised his voice to carry across the jurors to Shelton.

"What is your position with Adelaide's Breads, Inc. now?" Holt asked.

Shelton fingered his precisely knotted tie. "I became president when Miss Bailey became chairman of the board of directors."

Holt thought that was worth a little emphasis. Surely the jury would figure a "chairman of the board" type ought to be at least sane, if not sharp. He asked, "She actively presides at the directors' meeting?"

"She has . . . up to now," Shelton agreed.

Holt chewed his lower lip. A simple "yes" would have sufficed. He glanced at the jury.

The jurors looked wide-awake, even the tubby one. Holt decided to make short work of Shelton's opinion as to Adelaide's sanity and get on with the real fireworks.

Shelton swiveled back and forth in his chair.

Walking forward, Holt took a position by the end juror and stood silent until the witness settled down.

Then he made a jab with his trick pen, emphasizing the question: "Now, Mr. Shelton, based upon this long association, please tell the jury whether, in your opinion,

Adelaide Bailey is of sound or unsound mind."

Shelton answered in a monotone that carried no conviction.

"It is my opinion that Adelaide Bailey is of sound mind." He sounded like a small boy reciting lines he'd been made to memorize.

Holt muttered a "damn" under his breath. Why the hell couldn't Adelaide have left the man alone?

Then Shelton looked toward the jury box and gave a short, bitter laugh. "I better have that opinion — if I like my job."

Someone in the back of the courtroom sniggered. Furious, Holt started for the witness stand. His fist clenched so tight the ball point pen snapped in two.

Judge Woodruff raised his gavel. Recovering, Holt forced himself back to the bar rail that divided the courtroom. The jurors were watching curiously, expectantly.

Holt put both hands on the bar and gripped hard. It had been a close squeak. He'd damned near jumped Shelton and by so doing made the opposition a present of this witness's testimony, just as he had Doc's.

Woodruff cleared his throat impatiently. Holt knew he had to get on with it and try to salvage something from Shelton's testimony.

"That little aside you just volunteered," he challenged. "Was that because Miss Bailey rapped your knuckles? Or has that Dallas outfit offered you a job if you help them grab off Adelaide's Breads?"

Matthew Kane came to his feet in a swift movement. "I object," he thundered. "That's a leading question! And counsel's trying to impeach his own witness!"

Holt wheeled. "You couldn't be more right!"

Judge Woodruff cracked his gavel.

Holt faced toward the bench. "The witness has shown

57

himself to be hostile. I'm entitled to go after him like any hostile witness."

The judge checked further discussion with a rap of his gavel. "I'll sustain Mr. Kane's objection," he said.

Holt walked to the bench where further argument would be out of hearing of the jury. "Your Honor," he insisted, "that crack about his job could have no purpose except to keep the jury from believing him."

"The witness testified in your favor," Judge Woodruff pointed out. "I can't hold him hostile because he wasn't as convincing as you might like. Anyway, that's my ruling."

Shelton twisted in his chair, uncrossed and recrossed his legs. Judge Woodruff turned on him.

"Just keep to the questions," the judge growled.

Holt swore under his breath and glared at the witness. But Shelton returned a direct and unevasive look. The man had said nothing that wasn't true, Holt reminded himself. And anything he could wring out of a witness who'd acted hostile the jury would take as gospel truth.

The jurors had an attentive air about them as though they were eager to see whether the run-in with Shelton mightn't get hotter.

Holt took a few paces back from the witness stand and turned to face Shelton. "Do you know Reginald Bailey?" he asked.

"I do." Shelton spoke with reassuring definiteness.

"The young man who's brought this suit to have his aunt declared insane?"

Shelton nodded.

Across the table Kane began to gather himself, his tremendous frame straining forward, his hatchet-sized hands braced on the arms of his chair.

Ignoring these signs of an interruption at hand, Holt pushed on. "The young man who's petitioning to be put in

58

control of her business?"

"Objection!" Kane pushed himself to his feet. "The only question for the jury is whether Adelaide Bailey is of unsound mind. What to do about it, if she is, is a matter for the court. The question is irrelevant, immaterial . . ."

"Sustained." Judge Woodruff cut off the rest of the stock objection.

Holt wasted no time on an argument as to admissibility. Unanswered, the question served the purpose of being sure the jury knew Reg was in line to be Adelaide's guardian.

The jury looked to be getting the picture without difficulty. The juror next to the end said something to his tubby neighbor, who nodded understandingly. The lanky, sharp-looking chap in the foreman's seat was jackknifed forward with a finger cupping one ear.

Rummaging among his papers, Holt found a stubby pencil to take the place of the pen he'd snapped in two. He jabbed it toward Shelton.

"This same Reginald Bailey owns a thousand shares of Adelaide's Breads, Inc., doesn't he?"

Kane half rose, hesitated.

Shelton nodded. "He does. The other nine thousand are owned by his aunt."

Holt felt like beaming. His witness was ticking along now — hadn't paused to give Kane time to decide whether to object.

He shot his next question in quickly. "So this million dollar offer you've had for Adelaide Breads, Inc. would bring young Bailey a hundred thousand if he could put the deal over, right?"

"Objection!" Kane ejaculated, scrambling to his feet.

"Sustained!" Judge Woodruff snapped.

Holt smiled agreeably. "I admit the question was leading. I'll rephrase it." He would be glad, indeed, to put it five or six different ways for the jury.

"Hold it," Kane shouted.

At the same instant the judge's gavel cracked. "You gentlemen come up here," Judge Woodruff said dryly. "Perhaps we can keep a few matters that are not *for* the jury from being broadcast *to* the jury."

Kane and Holt raced for the bench as though the first there might whisper a secret word in the judge's ear. The judge waited until both were before him and turned to Holt.

"It wasn't the form of your question," the judge said. "I don't think the information asked for is admissible."

"Judge," Holt said, "I expect to prove Reg Bailey stands to get one hundred thousand . . ."

"Your question left small doubt as to that," Judge Woodruff cut in. "But you're getting the cart before the horse. First the *jury* decides if Adelaide Bailey is of unsound mind. If she is, *I* decide whether her next of kin is qualified to serve as guardian and what powers to give him."

"But your Honor," Holt argued, "I'm entitled to show Reg's motives for bringing this suit — what he stands to gain."

Judge Woodruff shook his head. "This isn't a civil suit between two parties. If Adelaide's worst enemy had filed the information that she's of unsound mind, it wouldn't make any difference. Either she's sane, or she's not and needs protection."

Holt stared at the judge in shocked disbelief. "Reg's motives make one hell of a difference," he blazed. "The difference in which way that jury will decide this case."

"I've made my ruling," the judge snapped. "I'll listen to testimony about Reginald Bailey when, as, and if I have to make an appointment of a guardian."

Stunned, Holt fell back a pace. Woodruff had gutted him. Small comfort that a higher court might have an opposite view of the law. Adelaide's strong pride and weak heart were unlikely to survive a judgment of insanity, however short-lived.

He opened his mouth to argue further. But the judge's ugly walleye had an unyielding look. Frustrated, Holt closed his mouth again and walked slowly back to his place.

Kane dropped into his chair with a clearly audible grunt of satisfaction. Holt checked the urge to heave a law book across the table and racked his brains for some way to win this jury over without bringing Adelaide into danger.

Now, across the table, Kane whispered something to Reggie.

Reg's heavy jowls shook in an appreciative giggle.

Holt eyed the heavy jowls, the trace of puffiness in the still prettyish face, the sag at the waist. Surely the jury hadn't missed these early marks of dedicated dissipation in Adelaide's precious nephew.

And, with the hints Holt had already given them, if the jury just knew about Reg's gambling debts, they'd have enough to form a pretty clear picture of what Reg was up to.

Judge Woodruff cleared his throat. His baleful glare demanded an end to delay.

Obviously his honor wasn't in a good humor. Probably he'd throw the book if Holt deliberately ignored that last ruling and made another effort to stigmatize Reg's motives. Certainly Woodruff had made it clear enough yesterday what he'd do if Holt got out of line again.

Considering matters, Holt got out of his chair and walked slowly to the far end of the jury box.

The judge let out a preparatory, "Harumph, . . ."

Quickly, nerving himself, Holt wheeled about and fired his question at the witness. "Just before young Bailey here brought this suit for control of his Aunt's fortune, wasn't he in your office begging for money to cover his gambling debts?"

Kane slammed the heel of a hatchet-like hand on the table. Holt felt the vibration from where he stood several yards away.

"Objection!" Kane roared, bursting out of his chair. His mane of hair shook. Some of it fell down in front of his angry red face, and he shoved it back impatiently. "Counsel's conduct is scandalous! A vicious, false attack on my client. A contemptuous violation of the court's ruling!"

Holt ignored the storm across the table and studied his jury. The reaction of the six men was all he could hope for.

The two chatty jurors in the center exchanged glances and turned speculative eyes on Reginald Bailey. Even the droopy-eyed tubby at the far end seemed to have been jarred awake.

But Holt watched most closely the lanky juror he'd picked as the likely foreman. That one kept his eyes fastened on Reg while he began a rapid-fire whisper to his neighbor.

Rubbing the corners of his mouth with thumb and forefinger, Holt concealed a small smile.

For the moment, he had forgotten Judge Woodruff. But the pounding of the judge's gavel demanded attention. Holt turned toward the bench. Old Glass-eye screwed his head to the right and shot a ghastly glare out of his lifeless eye. A glare that jarred Holt like an electric shock.

Then the judge swung his head back to survey the jury with his good eye. "Mr. Lawson's question is highly improper. Mr. Bailey has not given testimony. There is no reason to attack his character. As for his having brought this suit, gentlemen of the jury, if she is not competent, it would be your duty to find Miss Bailey of unsound mind, even if the devil himself had filed this petition. You can rest assured the court would appoint a proper guardian and closely supervise his administration of the estate."

Holt clenched his teeth. Old Glass-eye had let him have it.

Worse than a chewing-out. Practically invited the jury to find against him.

Shelton was still sitting up there with an attentive look on his face as though he expected more questions. Holt waved his hand in a disgusted gesture of dismissal and sank into his chair.

Now could he promise Adelaide the case was won? He looked from juror to juror, trying to read their thoughts. At the far end, Tubby looked blank. The two chatty jurors in the center were quiet at the moment, their eyes still on the judge, apparently disgesting his remarks.

Holt guessed these three didn't know where they stood. Not so the lanky, sharp-looking fellow in the foreman's seat. He was holding forth to his neighbor, apparently explaining the court's lecture. At one point he spread his hands, palms up, and shrugged.

That was enough for Holt. He saw what would happen in the jury room. The evidence *was* confusing as to whether Adelaide had reached an age where she needed protection. Now, with the judge's promise to name a qualified guardian and closely supervise his handling of the estate, the jury would ultimately agree on a finding that would insure Adelaide protection.

A finding that she was "of unsound mind."

Holt's skull filled with a great, violent ache. As always, the throbbing pain seemed to start and center where a pair of hostile football cleats had put the break in his nose.

Tugging at the crook, Holt tried to ease the pain so he could think better.

But what was there to think about? Hadn't Adelaide taken matters out of his hands? He remembered her standing in front of him that morning, her gaunt frame held proudly erect, declaring, "There's lots of things worse than dying."

Judge Woodruff's grating voice intruded. "All right, let's

get on, please."

It was a time for desperate measures. Drawing a deep, not wholly steady breath, Holt clamped his jaws together. Then he turned to Burgess.

"Go telephone Adelaide," he said. "Tell her to grab her nitroglycerin pills and get on down here. We're going to have to send in the first team."

Chapter 6

Burgess circled the counsel table and headed for the phone in the court clerk's office.

The throbbing in Holt's head hammered harder. The taut muscles of his jaw ached.

But the physical pain didn't hurt like the feeling of frustration and failure that racked him as he faced the necessity of endangering Adelaide's life.

Across the table Matthew Kane rose, squared his massive shoulders and grasped the lapels of his frock coat between fingers and thumb. He stood there, pompously erect, until he had every eye in the courtroom centered on him.

Picking up a legal pad, Holt forced himself to consider what tactics his opponent might adopt in the cross-examination of Shelton.

But Kane merely favored the witness with a broad smile and turned to the jury, grinning triumphantly. His tone insured that the most slow-witted juror should understand that Shelton's testimony had helped Kane's case.

"I have no questions to put to this witness," Kane boomed.

Holt tossed his pad back on the table. Trust Kane to select the most effective tactics of all. It seemed ages his antagonist stayed on his feet beaming on the jury, the spectators, the judge.

Then his eye came to rest on Holt. The glow changed to a cold glitter. Holt set his jaw. An involuntary quiver of revulsion touched him. Kane settled into his chair, still watching Holt. And while the smile stayed fixed, somehow it became an ugly thing.

Beneath the table, Holt balled his hands into fists and pounded them together. Now, even though he hated for Adelaide to have to go through it, he began to look forward to the pleasure of seeing that sneer wiped off Kane's face when she made her appearance.

Judge Woodruff excused the witness with a gesture. Then he swiveled back to face Holt. "Does that conclude your evidence, Mr. Lawson?" he demanded.

Holt tensed his muscles and got to his feet. "No, Your Honor, I have one more witness. She's on her way now. Adelaide Bailey!"

A collective gasp sounded in the courtroom. On the other side of the table Reg jackknifed forward, and his plump chin bobbled as he whispered excitedly in Kane's ear.

In spite of his misgivings about Adelaide's appearance, Holt couldn't help but enjoy the consternation it was causing in the enemy camp.

Kane waved Reg off and shot to his feet. "Your Honor," he began, "I object to . . ."

"Just a minute!" Judge Woodruff interrupted. He faced the jury. "You gentlemen go ahead and take your morning recess now."

As the jurors filed out, the judge turned back to the counsel table. "Now if you gentlemen will come up here, I think we can discuss this matter privately."

Holt let Kane precede him. Following deliberately, he debated what his wily antagonist was going to try to pull.

In front of the bench Kane wheeled on Holt, his face

66

flushed. "What is this? You filed an affidavit Adelaide was too sick to appear. You needed more time . . . she couldn't be examined . . . Was all that perjury?"

Holt ignored his opponent and addressed himself to the judge. "Adelaide's got a weak heart, all right. But she's got a strong head. She's made up her mind she's coming down here and put an end to this nonsense."

Kane flushed; swung back to face the court. "There must be some precedent for stopping this sort of thing," he protested. "Holt oughtn't be allowed to risk a woman's life — just because he's afraid of losing the retainers he's wheedled out of her."

Involuntarily Holt took a step toward Kane — fists clenched, control teetering. Then he checked himself and slowly straightened his fingers. He had Kane on the ropes, and he wasn't going to let the old shyster trick him into a mistrial.

"I just don't know, Holt . . ." Judge Woodruff began.

"Judge," Holt said, "Adelaide's on her way down here. If you have any idea of keeping her off the stand, you'll have to tell her so yourself."

The judge considered that suggestion with the look of a man who'd bit into a particularly sour apple. "She's still running her affairs," he said shortly. "She can testify if she wants to."

Kane shook his head. "It's not right, Judge. Either that affidavit of Holt's was downright perjury or she shouldn't take the stand."

Remembering Kane's tactics, Holt had a sudden qualm. He faced his adversary. "You listen to me, Kane. That affidavit was true enough that you just better not start any of your fireworks."

"That's right, Matthew," Judge Woodruff chimed in. "I'm not going to stand for any rough stuff."

"Of course I'll go easy with her, Judge," Kane promised.

Holt felt his tension ease. Only then Kane turned and levelled an accusing finger. "Just you remember though, Holt," he warned, "I tried to keep her off the stand. Now if anything happens, it'll be on your head, not mine!"

From just inside the south entrance to the courthouse, Holt watched the point where Elm Street came into the square. He wished this next hour were over, both for Adelaide and for himself.

Then the big familiar, black limousine wheezed out of Elm Street. Holt crossed the courthouse lawn to meet Adelaide.

She descended from her car and paused, straightening the folds of her long skirt. Then, adjusting her flowered, bucket-shaped hat, she felt the button of her high-necked blouse.

Holt smiled. Old-fashioned she might be. But even more, she was queenly.

Taking a grip on her cane, she started for the courthouse door. Holt reached for her arm, reminding himself not to show surprise at her fraility. Even so, the feel of her thinness worried him.

"Is Doc coming down?" Holt asked, not letting her move as fast as she tried.

"I didn't tell him." She gestured with a big tapestry bag she carried. "All he knows is to pop a pill under my tongue if I have a spell."

"But, — couldn't Miss Phoebe come with you?"

"Wouldn't let her," Adelaide replied firmly. "She was all in a dither."

Holt frowned — felt a small, quiet chill at the responsibility of having Adelaide alone for the ordeal ahead. But at least Burgess would be there.

The thought comforted him. Together Adelaide and he went slowly but steadily up the granite stairs. As best he could, he steered her around the hollow places in the steps that numberless footsteps had worn. You couldn't have a marriage, a birth, a death, in Pinewood County without a trip to the courthouse. Vengeance, greed, ambition, and fear had all driven litigants up these stairs. The grooves in the steps marked their path. And from the roof, the red gargoyles put there by a mocking architect grinned down upon the motley human procession.

As they walked toward the elevator, Adelaide squeezed Holt's arm. "Many's the time your dad and I went to the mat with some'un or other in here."

Remembering the cases he'd watched his father try, Holt wished the old boy were with him now.

Adelaide continued as though thinking out loud. "You're still coltish, but durned if I don't believe you're gonna turn out a tougher customer than he was."

Holt chuckled. "That's quite a compliment, coming from you." Maneuvering Adelaide into the elevator, he started it creaking slowly toward the floor of Judge Woodruff's courtroom, then turned to Adelaide.

A vial of pills lay half concealed in her hand. Breathing heavily, eyes half closed, she leaned hard on her cane. Concerned, yet feeling completely helpless, Holt endured the elevator's long slow journey. When it stopped, he held it stationary with the door grill open, waiting for Adelaide's spell to pass.

Gradually, her respiration became more regular. She dropped the vial of pills into her purse and snapped the big bag shut. Holt took a deep breath of his own.

"This is silly, Adelaide," he protested. "I'm going to get hold of Kane and pay off."

"No. I didn't even have to take a pill." For another few

69

moments she rested on her cane. Then her eyes opened wide.

"A woman ought to marry," she said. "All I'll leave is a way for other women to have their kids. That's what the jobs at the plant do." Her bony hand gripped Holt's arm. "Don't let anything happen to it, Holt."

"We'll talk about it after the trial," he promised, patting the hand. "Maybe I'll whip up a codicil fixing it so Townsend couldn't sell it."

Adelaide's thin lips twisted in a sneer. "I wouldn't trust either of the Townsends far as I'd chase a skunk. You're the one I'm looking to, boy."

She gripped her cane and marched forward.

Worried, Holt released the elevator door and watched it swing to. Adelaide's memory wouldn't stand up to much questioning this morning. Obviously she didn't remember her will named Townsend's bank the trustee of her estate.

And she must be feeling like hell. Even more than the pill he'd caught her on the verge of using, that conversation about babies and dying told him. A hale Adelaide would be sounding "charge" on her bugle, not "hearts and flowers."

He went after her and took her past the crowded courtroom entrance and through the clerk's office.

As Holt and Adelaide approached the counsel table, Reg hunched forward, eyes fixed on the floor, only his red hair and back of his brown silk coat visible. Not so Kane. Getting his six foot four up with a surprising swiftness, swinging the heavy oak chairs like toy stools, he cleared a path.

"Good morning, Adelaide," he said, injecting the tenderest concern into his salutation.

Adelaide ignored him, her eyes on Reg. It jarred him into action. He hurried over. "Good morning, Aunt Adelaide."

Holt's stomach protested the syrupy, pseudo-filial smile. But Adelaide accepted the arm Reg proffered. And now Kane had the gall to take Adelaide's other arm and help her toward the witness box.

Dumbfounded, Holt watched the precious pair enact a skit obviously contrived to demonstrate to the jury their solicitude for Adelaide.

Feeling outmaneuvered, Holt circled the counsel table and sat down beside Brugess. "You've got to hand it to Kane," he said in an undertone. "He knows he's through, now that Adelaide's here. But he struts his stuff to the bitter end."

Judge Woodruff leaned across his bench toward Adelaide. "The witness will please raise her right hand," he said.

Adelaide turned and looked up at the judge's dais for the first time. "Why, good morning, Waldemar," she said.

"Good morning, Adelaide." Judge Woodruff's mouth worked as though trying to identify an unexpected flavor. "Will you raise your right hand, please?"

An intense stillness settled over the courtroom as the judge administered the oath.

Then Holt felt as though the spotlight suddenly had swung to center on him. He faced toward Adelaide. "Please state your name," he said.

Adelaide looked over at the jury box. "If there's any of you don't know by now I'm Adelaide Bailey, we ought to change places."

Holt stretched his mouth in a wide smile and turned to Burgess, nodding appreciation of Adelaide's humor. That the turn was toward the jury was simple reflex. Had Adelaide sounded quaint or queer? Ninety percent of the courtroom would accept the first label put on it. Holt hastened to furnish his.

The lean juror in the seat that would ultimately belong to the foreman smiled back at Adelaide. The two chatty jurors in the center exchanged amused glances.

Satisfied, Holt nodded and turned back. So far, so good.

But he wanted no continuation of her sparring. Encouraged, Adelaide could get way out. Instead of laughing with her, people would laugh at her.

He got a tone of no-nonsense-now-and-I-mean-it to his voice. "For the record, Miss Bailey, please identify yourself."

"All right," Adelaide replied, smiling at him. "I'm Adelaide Bailey, 88, old maid, born and raised right here in Pinewood."

"You are the founder of the company known as Adelaide's Breads, Inc.?"

"Started it in my own kitchen."

"It has been successful?"

Adelaide nodded her head vigorously. "Of the folks that work in Pinewood, half or better have jobs with us. Baking breads and cakes 'round the clock. We sell all over East Texas."

Holt picked up his stub of a pencil and toyed with it. If he had known it would come to putting Adelaide on the stand, he would have gone over the next questions with her. Made sure their meaning and purpose were clear.

Good Lord, he thought, you can use the naughty word when you're talking to yourself. You'd have coached her but good.

He took a deep breath and let it escape slowly along with a prayer. "Now, Miss Bailey, do you understand the nature of the proceedings here this morning?"

"Of course I do!" Her voice rose shrilly. "They're trying to tear down everything I've done. They're . . ."

"Adelaide!" Holt cut off her tirade, simultaneously cursing himself for getting stampeded into putting her on the stand without proper preparation. All right, dammit, coaching. Spouting off like that with no preliminaries made her sound dotty. Perspiration popped out under his arms and began to trickle down his body. "Now, Adelaide, I asked you . . ."

Matthew Kane was on his feet. His stentorian voice drowned out Holt's. "Let the witness answer the question," he boomed. "The kind of answer she makes, whatever it may be, reflects her understanding or lack of it."

Judge Woodruff rapped his gavel and turned to Adelaide. "You may proceed," he said.

Holt hunched forward in his chair, his hands clasped together. He focused his eyes on Adelaide, trying to communicate a warning to her. She gave him a nod.

"I know what you asked me," she said. She pointed a long, thin finger at Reginald Bailey. "That young whippersnapper I raised is trying to have me declared insane so he can get hold of my property. I've footed my last bill for his drunken gambling sprees."

There might well have been a missle launching across the table. Kane came out of his chair like a rocket, and a second later his roar blasted Holt's ears. "Objection! That's irrelevant, incompetent, immaterial. It's an obvious attempt to create prejudice against my client. Hasn't any foundation in fact."

He swiveled toward Holt, a sneer on his face. "The witness seems to have been well coached!"

Holt felt the heat of blood rushing to his face. He leaned across the table, an angry retort ready. But at that instant Judge Woodruff cleared his throat. Holt glanced at the judge. Woodruff's good eye was watching him with a neutral curiosity.

Turning back, Holt caught a look of calculation behind Kane's sneer. It put him instantly on guard. Abandoning the angry retort, he cast about in his mind for argument for admitting Adelaide's reply. Inspiration. He compressed his lips as he got to his feet.

"Let the witness answer the question." He mimicked

Kane's tone as well as his words. "The kind of reply she makes, whatever it may be, reflects her understanding or lack of it."

Judge Woodruff had a wry smile on his face as he nodded to Adelaide. "You may proceed," he said.

Adelaide looked at Reginald Bailey, and her face lost some of its sternness. "I don't blame the boy," she said gently. "He was frightened and needed money. They showed him how he could get it by selling my plant to an outfit that just wants my markets."

A quiet gripped the courtroom. Holt could hear her heavy breathing. The jury had the picture now, and no one could question that Adelaide knew what was what. He waved his hand in a satisfied gesture of dismissal and turned to Kane. "Your witness," he said.

Adelaide swiveled her chair, and her eye followed Holt's to Kane. Her look changed to a glare.

"The boy's got a whole pack of jackals running with him now," she observed. "They're all panting for a share of the carcass."

Judge Woodruff gave his desk a short rap with his gavel. "Adelaide!"

"Yes, Waldemar?"

Judge Woodruff opened his mouth, closed it, and let matters go with a shake of his head.

Holt forced himself not to smile.

The courtroom quieted, waiting for Kane to begin his cross examination. Again Holt heard Adelaide's heavy breathing, more labored than before, it seemed to him. Beneath that peppery front she put on, she was feeling the strain. Disturbed, he looked across the table at Kane.

His adversary was studying the jury. Bushy white eyebrows knit, the big lawyer moved piercing blue eyes slowly from juror to juror. With the heel of his right hand, he beat a tattoo on the table as another man would do with his fingers.

Holt knew that now Kane would read only bad news in the jurors' faces. Every week, Adelaide's Bread's paymaster presented a golden egg to Pinewood County. No East Texas jury would deliver that goose to Dallas to be killed. Anyway, didn't Adelaide, for all of her peculiarities, take better care of her money than Reginald?

Adelaide's breathing became more regular. But Holt saw her clutch her purse more closely, and he knew she was thinking of the box of nitroglycerin pills inside.

He leaned across the table. "Remember now, Kane, you go easy with her."

Kane turned. His eyes glittered with an unnatural brightness. Holt had the feeling that no warmth, no emotion, lay beneath that diamond hardness.

"And you remember that it was you who put her on the stand," Kane said coldly.

Holt didn't like that answer. He gripped the arms of his chair, readying himself. If Kane got rough, Holt planned to bounce in with objections and take the heat off Adelaide. Then he'd needle his antagonist until Kane turned his fire on Holt.

But Kane sat relaxed in his chair and put his first question in a gentle voice. "Reginald is your only blood kin?"

Adelaide nodded.

"Your dead brother's child?"

Adelaide nodded again. Her eyes turned to Reg, who sat humped over, staring at the floor.

Kane glanced at Reg and back to Adelaide. "Now I believe you said Reginald had lost money gambling."

Curious, Holt turned to study Kane. He'd expected Kane's last desperate try would be to rattle Adelaide, make

75

her appear confused. Why was his opponent doing Holt the favor of hammering into the jury's mind the matter of Reg's gambling?

Again Adelaide shook her head in the affirmative.

"And Reginald came to you and asked you for money to pay those debts, but you denied him?" Kane asked.

Adelaide's chin jutted forward a trifle. "Reginald's got to learn to stand on his own two feet sometime." Holt could detect no worsening in her breathing. As promised, so far Kane had gone easy with her.

Kane softened his tone even more. "Did Reginald tell you those gamblers had threatened to kill him?"

"I didn't believe that." Adelaide's voice lost some of its firmness.

Kane's voice stayed soft, but now a note of incredulity crept into it. "You mean you kept that full purse of yours snapped shut? You risked their leaving your brother's son a riddled, rotting corpse sprawled in some gutter?"

"He'd said that sort of thing before," Adelaide muttered. A grayness dulled her cheeks. Against it the touch of color she'd put on was an ugly blotch. Holt thrust himself out of his chair. "Your honor, . . ." he protested.

At the same instant, Judge Woodruff cracked his gavel. "Mr. Kane!" he rebuked. "Mr. Kane!"

Heedless, Kane came out of his chair like a boxer at the bell and stalked to the witness box. Pulling himself to his full height, he pointed an accusing finger down at Adelaide. His body shook. His shock of gray hair rumpled. His voice rumbled like an angry, avenging prophet.

"Our Lord said, 'If he trespass against thee seven times in a day, and seven times in a day turn again to thee, saying, I repent; thou shalt forgive him.' But you gave no heed to the words of our Lord. You hardened your heart against your own blood."

For a moment Adelaide glared. She half raised her cane.

Then a grimace of pain contorted her face. She clutched at her chest with her right hand and bent forward. Her ragged breathing rasped through the courtroom.

Holt started for the witness stand. He sensed Burgess coming right behind him.

But Kane was already at the witness stand, and his demeanor changed abruptly. Leaning across the rail that enclosed the witness box, he reached for the big tapestry bag and opened it. "You need one of your pills, Adelaide," he said solicitously.

Holt felt Burgess's hands on his back. "Let me get to her," Burgess urged.

He stepped aside and pushed Burgess forward.

Kane held the open purse in his left hand and a vial of pills in his right.

"I'll do that," Burgess said sharply. She grasped Kane's hand that held the vial and shook the little white disks into her palm. Her hands trembled, and a number of pellets fell into the purse; but she got hold of one and slipped it under Adelaide's tongue.

Holt breathed a sigh of relief. He'd seen Adelaide recover from an angina attack in moments . . . as soon as the nitroglycerin enlarged the arteries and let more blood to the heart.

But Adelaide didn't react that way. Holt watched her eyes widen as though startled, fearful. She opened her mouth. He bent forward to hear what she was trying to say. But she managed only a feeble groan.

Now Holt pushed past Kane and put his arms around Adelaide's thin frame in such a way as to give her head support. She felt cold, clammy with perspiration. He pulled his handkerchief out and wiped the sweat from her forehead.

"You'll be all right," he said.

She turned to him. Now he saw in her eyes and in her face an emotion he had never associated with Adelaide — fear.

Then her eyes rolled upward. Holt saw she no longer recognized him. A lifeless grayness spread from Adelaide's face into her hands. Suddenly she sat bolt upright. A gasp racked her body.

Desperately, Holt tried to brace her. Burgess assisted from the other side. But the next instant Adelaide collapsed in their arms. For a moment paralysis froze Holt. Then, in frantic haste, he picked Adelaide's pitifully light body up, carried her to the judge's office, and laid her on the couch.

Deep in Adelaide's throat a grating noise sounded. Each deep gasp came more slowly. Still she fought to suck in the life-giving air.

Holt took her cold hands in his and tried to massage some warmth into them. A check in her breathing startled him. Then a noisy, rattling gasp. Not knowing, he felt a surge of hope at the new sound. But afterwards there was only silence.

Awkwardly, he tried to find her pulse beat. Tried and failed.

Judge Woodruff came into the office. "The ambulance is on the way," he said.

Holt shook his head wordlessly. Making his way around the judge's desk, he swung the high-backed chair about so he was concealed. For a few moments he sat there, head in his hands. A suffocating tightness squeezed his chest and throat. Then — spasmodically, involuntarily — a sudden great sob shook his body. The tears he had choked back streamed down his face. The tightness eased, letting him pull in a great breath.

Once he thought he heard a sound from the couch. He wheeled around and was at Adelaide's side in two quick strides. But the lifeless fixity of her body, the waxy grayness of her face, told him instantly his mind had played him a trick.

The woman who had both mothered and fathered him was dead.

Chapter 7

Holt slumped forward in the judge's chair, his hands clasped together, his head resting on the cool steel top of the judge's strong box.

Letting the tears come for a moment had relieved the choking feeling. Breathing more freely, he shut off the waterworks.

Adelaide had been a fighter. Her hooked nose and out-thrust chin could have belonged to an ungentle Cossack. And she and Holt had admired in each other a quality of toughness that seemed to be going out of style.

Turning away, Holt set his jaw. A few tears wouldn't square accounts with Adelaide. He owed it to her to finish this trouble. Damned if Reg was going to sell the plant and poop off the proceeds after what she'd been through! And Adelaide would spin in her grave if Holt allowed Kane to get fat on fees out of her estate while her murder went unavenged.

Standing, he began to pace. He had to get to Townsend before Reg persuaded the banker to do anything shortsighted as Adelaide's executor and trustee. He'd have to convince the old man that what was good for Adelaide's Breads was good for Banker Townsend.

At the couch Holt paused and looked down. Against the

waste of Adelaide's face, her forehead appeared higher and broader as though it had had to expand to house a giant intelligence.

Remembering her steel trap mind, Holt dismissed a nagging thought. Adelaide just couldn't have messed up the will that blueprinted how her enterprises were to be carried on. Reg must have been lying to Townsend when he said she had.

A sound out in the courtroom interrupted his chain of thought. Rapid footsteps seemed to be coming toward the judge's office.

Holt gave his eyes a swipe with his handkerchief and faced the door.

Joe White dashed in and unslung an oxygen kit that hung over the shoulder of his coat.

Holt shook his head. "She's dead, Joe," he said.

An older man came through the door, panting. Joe White turned to him. "Better check, Dad."

George White pulled a stethoscope out of the pocket of his dark business suit, inserted the ear pieces and held the other end against Adelaide's chest.

Crossing to the desk, Holt sat on its front edge and watched. Burgess, Kane, Reg and the judge formed a knot at the door and, one by one, filtered in.

After a few seconds, George White stood up. "You're right, Holt. No need Doc's coming."

Father and son straightened their ties and shrugged away the rumpled appearance of their identical dark suits. Holt recognized the transition from ambulance attendants to funeral directors.

"Shall we take charge of the body?" George White asked.

Their ready attention to business grated on Holt's already raw nerves. Miss Phoebe ought to have the say, but Holt didn't want to tell her of Adelaide's death by phone. He hesitated.

On the other hand, Kane lost no time. He whispered something to Reg.

"You go right ahead, George," Reg piped up.

Holt started. Thinking about Miss Phoebe, he'd forgotten Adelaide's precious nephew. But Kane had moved fast to establish his client's position as legal next of kin. Scowling, Holt turned his attention back to the Whites.

George White crossed to the couch and leaned over Adelaide's body. With swift efficiency, he stripped off her rings and watch and removed a brooch from her breast.

"Where's her pocketbook?" White asked.

Holt looked around. Burgess had the oversized purse. So Burgess, not Reg or Kane, had held it while Adelaide was dying.

Holt moderated his scowling. Somehow it made him feel better that Burgess, who was genuinely fond of Adelaide, had held the bag. A woman's purse was an intimate thing.

Burgess handed the big tapestry bag to George White. As she turned back, Holt caught her eye and beckoned. She came across the room.

"Can you go on out to Miss Phoebe's?" Holt asked. "I better stick around here for now. Tell her I'll be there quick as I can."

Burgess nodded and left the room. Holt turned to watch George White. The mortician had Adelaide's purse opened. Swiftly, like a butcher wrapping chicken he'd just gutted, he packed away Adelaide's jewelry.

Finished, he snapped the purse shut. Holt winced.

Then a clicking sounded and Joe White wheeled in a stretcher. Father and son swung the long, emaciated body from couch to stretcher. Startled, Holt realized they were ready to go.

There was a strangeness to the proceedings. Adelaide had

lived over eighty years in Pinewood. Her life had touched nearly every person in the community. How could it take but a few seconds to ready her to be wheeled away forever?

Holt half raised his arm to check their haste; but for what purpose he could not think, and he let his arm drop to his side.

George White picked up Adelaide's purse and gestured with it. "Who should I give this to?" he asked.

Kane stepped forward and fastened on to the bag. "We'll take that," he said.

Caught unaware, Holt watched the purse grabbed by the man whose third degree had killed Adelaide, saw it clutched in hands stained with Adelaide's blood.

Anger surged in him, beyond all logic. Exploding into action, he reached out, snatched the bag from Kane, and settled back on the desk.

Kane's mouth dropped open. Then, giant of a man that he was, he set his jaw, flattened his hands into thin hatchets, and advanced.

Holt shoved the tapestry bag to a safe place well behind him. Happily balling his hands into fists, he pushed off the desk and raised his guard. He felt almost grateful to his broad-shouldered adversary. It was accommodating of Kane to offer such an early opportunity to make payment on account for Adelaide.

Kane edged nearer. Exulting, Holt set himself to batter that smooth, hypocritical face.

But Judge Woodruff let out a bellow, "Matthew!!!"

The volume and violence of the runty judge got through to Holt even in his heat of excitement.

Kane stopped in his tracks.

Now the bantam jurist stalked to the middle of the room and glared up at Kane. "Sit down," he barked.

Kane backed into one of the low leather chairs.

The judge's baleful walleye sought out Holt. With an effort, Holt got himself back to the desk and leaned against it, breathing hard. Puffed up like a banty rooster, the diminutive judge strutted across the room.

Holt saw that his honor wanted his perch. Sweeping up Adelaide's bag, Holt tucked it firmly under his arm and squatted on the edge of the couch.

Judge Woodruff installed himself on the desk top and fixed his left eye on Kane. "My court is not going to be run on the lines of a barroom brawl," he declared. "Not if I have to get somebody's license lifted. Is that clear?"

"I'm sorry, Your Honor, really sorry." Kane sounded really sorry.

The judge's mild brown eye took over operations. Holt made note of the effectiveness of Kane's kowtowing and wondered if he could stomach using the technique.

Then Kane gave Holt a rancorous look and turned back to the judge. "It just made my blood boil though, Judge. Holt killed Adelaide, dragging her down here. And the minute she's gone, all he thinks about is grabbing on to her jewelry."

Holt felt his face flush with anger. But this time he didn't let his temper distract him. He wanted to know why Kane was so hell bent on getting hold of Adelaide's purse.

Taking it from under his arm, Holt hefted it thoughtfully. The big bag had an amazing weight and bulk for a frail woman to have lugged about. Most of that weight and bulk, Holt knew, came from the stack of notebooks Adelaide always carried.

If Reg didn't actually know what Adelaide had done about her will, could Kane be wanting to sift those notes for a clue?

"How about it, Holt?" Judge Woodruff questioned. "Shouldn't the purse go to her only kin?"

83

Holt decided to play it as though he accepted the jewelry as the object of interest. He dangled the tapestry bag in front of him. "No," he replied. "Reg doesn't get this to hock. His gambler friends are going to have to wait and wait for their money."

Reg paled and looked to Kane.

"How do you get that way?" Kane demanded.

"There's a copy of her will in my files. Dad was to have been her executor and trustee. Now that he's dead, it's the bank."

"But surely her personal effects . . ." Kane began.

"Go to Miss Phoebe," Holt concluded firmly. "Everything of value goes into the trust. Reg gets a monthly income."

He turned to Adelaide's pudgy nephew. "How about it, Reg?" he taunted. "Can you talk Fox into a long, long pay out?"

Reg twisted jerkily in his seat. Clasping his hands together, he steadied them on his knee. "That will's ancient history," he blurted. "Aunt Adelaide . . ."

Kane gave his head an almost imperceptible shake. Holt caught the gesture out of the corner of his eye. Reg clammed up.

Judge Woodruff exhaled impatiently and walked around the desk to his strong box. "Give me the purse," he said.

Holt was still wondering about the exchange between Kane and Reg. His thoughts absorbed, he sat dangling the big tapestry bag in front of him.

The judge swung around and shot an impatient glance through his whitish eye. "Do you want an order in writing? The purse goes into my safe — until I name someone to handle the estate."

Snapping out of his reverie, Holt handed over the bag. Judge Woodruff stuffed it into his safe and secured the door.

"I won't have room for another damned thing," he grumbled.

"We'd all be better off to find out where we are," Kane declared. "I say, let's look in her safety deposit box. If she had a will, it's there."

Holt liked the suggestion. Knowing Adelaide, he'd bet his bottom dollar they'd find a will. But aloud he said, "Keep your shirt on. She isn't even in her grave yet."

Kane shook his head. "If there's no will, I want to file an application by day after tomorrow. That way notice will run in time for the court to appoint my client administrator a week from Monday."

"You're in a hell of a hurry," Holt commented.

"This offer for Adelaide's Breads won't stay open forever," Kane retorted.

Holt raised his eyebrows and shrugged, disassociating himself from the unseemly haste.

Judge Woodruff, in turn, looked from Kane to Holt and back as though expecting more than such minimal wrangling. Then he spread his hands. "If there's no real objection, I'll issue an order for the box to be opened."

Holt got up with careful casualness. "I'll wander over to the bank and get us a room to work in. We'll need Adelaide's key."

"She always carried that key in her purse," Reg asserted. And Kane barked, "Don't you go into that box without us!"

"How the hell could I?" Holt snapped and turned to the judge. "Your Honor, you won't let anybody go into that purse except yourself, will you?"

Judge Woodruff shook his head.

Holt sauntered through the courtroom into the corridor. Once out of sight, he tore off for Townsend's office. Cutting across the courthouse lawn, he made for the one-story building with the heavily barred windows and granite block walls that advertised the bank's sturdiness.

Inside the bank, Connie's father, a small, wiry man, sat at the far end of the lobby in a cubicle with glass partitions through which he kept an eye on the line of tellers' cages.

Holt acknowledged the greetings of the bank clerks with a quick nod and hurried back into a hall and through the door marked, "President".

Townsend looked up and frowned. Holt crossed the room and thrust his hand across the desk. Townsend gave it a quick, nervous shake.

Ignoring the leather chair placed so as to keep the wide desk between the banker and would-be borrowers, Holt dragged a wooden straight chair across the cork floor and placed it at Townsend's elbow.

The banker pushed back in his chair. Sharp eyes, set close together in a narrow face, took on a guarded look.

"I'm meeting Kane and Reg to look for Adelaide's will," Holt said.

Townsend nodded without comment.

"I'm sure Dad gave you a copy," Holt continued. "The bank will be executor and trustee."

The wizened little man shook his head. "She revoked that will. Reginald said so."

"Horsefeathers! Reg bluffed you," Holt declared. "He hashed up every job Adelaide ever gave him. She wouldn't leave things so he could do it again."

Townsend's mouth dropped open. After a few moments he ran his tongue over his lips and slowly closed them.

Holt waited until the idea had time to sink in. Then he snapped out a question: "Did you make a deal with Reg?"

The other's close-set eyes got the chill blue of a banker about to turn down a loan.

"Now, look," Holt protested, "we don't have much time. You're Connie's dad. I want to go the way that there's the most in it for you."

Townsend pursed his lips. "Reginald's been like one of the family. With both of us owing sizeable amounts, — well, of course, we've had some talks."

Holt gave Townsend an understanding nod. "The smart thing would have been to agree to work together to sell the plant and get both of you out of the hole, no matter what set of circumstances came up."

Townsend's silence admitted he'd done the smart thing.

Holt picked up a pencil and pad from the desk and began doodling. "But with Adelaide dead and you in the driver's seat, that'd just be peanuts for you."

"Peanuts!" Townsend exclaimed. "Holt, I owe upwards of $50,000."

Holt nodded and earnestly jotted down random figures. "Like I said, peanuts," he affirmed. "Hope you didn't put anything in writing."

"Course I didn't." Townsend put on a pair of specs and scrutinized Holt's scribblings. After a moment he shrugged, pulled his glasses off and looked at Holt inquiringly.

"Between us, we could handle the directors," Holt said. "Get that raise through you've been wanting."

"It's too late now," Townsend sighed. "I need that $50,000 P. D. Q."

Holt shrugged. "No problem there. We can put through a loan for you if we jump your income. Another thing, with Adelaide gone, the bakery corporation ought to retain a financial consultant. Why not you?"

Townsend looked dazed. Then he picked up a pencil and began making jottings of his own.

Holt crossed the fingers of his left hand and tapped the wood leg of the chair. "Three or four years and you'd be square. But that income would go on and on."

Busy with his figures, Townsend nodded.

Holt decided he'd fed the old man enough carrots and

now was time for the stick. He gestured with his pad of figures.

"Without the baking plant, this burg would fold. You'd lose fifty thousand dollars on that house of yours alone."

Townsend started. Then something in the lobby seemed to catch his eye. He watched for a moment, pulled his sheet of figures from the pad and wadded it into a ball that he dropped into the wastebasket.

Turning, Holt saw Kane and Reg coming toward them. He stood, "Looks like we've got a quorum. Okay to use the directors' room?"

"Of course." Townsend got up and led the way. Reginald and Kane joined them in the hall and they filed into a carpeted room with a long table of gleaming walnut.

Kane walked to the far end and pulled out one of the handsome black leather arm chairs. Seating himself, he waved to Townsend. "Let Reg and Holt go get the box," he said. "I want to talk to you."

Holt pricked up his ears. Reluctantly he left Kane and Townsend in conference.

As best he could, he rushed the vault custodian through the formalities. Finally, flat steel box in hand and Reg close on his heels, he hurried back to the directors' room.

Kane sat where Holt had left him, his brows pulled down in a scowl. Townsend had abandoned his chair and was making quick, nervous turns about the room.

"Yes, yes. I understand, Matthew," Townsend jerked out. "I'll get my trust committee together. But some of them . . . Well, asking them to close the plant . . ."

Holt felt a tingle at the corners of his mouth. Townsend was giving Kane the old run-around.

Repressing a smile, Holt let the safety deposit box clatter onto the table. Townsend jumped, then abandoned his conversation with obvious relief. Kane scrambled out of his chair and took up guard duty on Holt's left. Reg and Townsend positioned themselves a Holt's right. Reg's breath smelled of stale cigarettes, and Townsend began a nervous sniffing.

Holt looked left and right at the three heads bunched around him. "Everybody ready?" he asked dryly.

Agreement.

Holt lifted the metal lid. A folded instrument lay by itself in the bottom of the box. Holt regonized the familiar form of blue back cover bearing his father's name and address. Typed across the outside were the words, "Last will and testament of Adelaide Bailey."

Wordless, Holt picked up the document; displayed it.

"What are you trying to pull, Holt?" Kane sputtered. "Let me see that."

Holt moved the will back out of reach. "What did you expect?" he chortled. "That she'd turn her businesses over to a chump who couldn't keep his check book balanced?" Then, holding it so all could see, he turned the pages. Slowly at first, so all could read the legacies to church and charity, the provisions for home and income to Miss Phoebe.

Then he came to routine stuff, the standard, lengthy boiler plate that lawyers use to set up a trust; and he began to flick the pages more quickly.

A hand — Townsend's — clapped him on the shoulder.

Finally, the last page turned up.

Or rather, part of the last page. Because someone had neatly torn out Adelaide's signature.

And below the tear, at the bottom of the page in Adelaide's unmistakable large, firm handwriting was inscribed one brief, paralyzing sentence:

"I hereby revoke this will.

Adelaide Bailey"

Chapter 8

Holt had the feeling that comes when a tackle's arms have closed around your ankles and you're waiting for the ground to thrust up and knock the wind out of you. Stunned, he hunched deep in the high-backed leather chair . . . eyed dully the blue backed paper on which he'd pinned his hopes — the will Adelaide had revoked.

At some time in the past Kane had crowed triumphantly and strutted out with Reg and Townsend at his heels. Had it been moments ago? An hour? Holt didn't know, didn't care.

At the head of the table stood the chair in which Adelaide had been accustomed to preside, Holt at her side. Even now Kane was probably busy with the papers that would ensconce himself and Reg in those seats. Holt felt his lips twist in a sardonic grin, tasted the bitterness.

The chair became uncomfortable. Standing, he went to stare disconsolately out the window. In the distance wisps of smoke curled upward from Adelaide's plant. So how about a few tears for the workers out there while he was crying in his beer?

Turning from the window, Holt began to pace. Even now, he found it hard to believe Adelaide had botched up the blueprint she'd devised to insure that those things dear to her were carried on. She hadn't been that weak-minded, that doting. This very morning she'd stood before him like a queen and issued her orders with an iron will.

The safety deposit box still rested on the table beside the blue backed paper. Picking up the voided will, Holt tossed it into the empty box.

It looked lost in the otherwise vacant container.

Holt stiffened . . .

Where were the certificates for Adelaide's bank stock? Her bakery stock? Where were all the other things she would have accumulated? War bonds? Cast-off jewelry? Blood pounded in Holt's veins. Adelaide had cleaned out this box. This voided will was here only because she'd junked it. When he found the rest of her valuables, he'd find her actual will also!

Relief and new hope so exhilarated him that he had to get a grip on himself to attack the problem of where Adelaide might have cached her movable assets.

His watch put the time at a little after noon. Burgess and Miss Phoebe would have eaten. If he rushed on out to Adelaide's house, Miss Phoebe and he could make the necessary trip to the funeral home. And he'd have a chance to ask Adelaide's closest confidante where to look for the vital papers.

Leaving the safety deposit box where it lay, Holt hurried to his car. At the door of Adelaide's house, Burgess, bless her, met him and reported.

Burgess had broken the news of Adelaide's death. So far Miss Phoebe hadn't given way even to the extent of a few tears. With her customary foresight, Adelaide had left instructions as to the dress she should be buried in. Burgess had both Miss Phoebe and Adelaide's things ready to go to the funeral home.

Holt helped Miss Phoebe out to his station wagon. He hoped, on the way, to get the conversation around to what

Adelaide might have done with the contents of her safety deposit box.

But there was no conversation. Miss Phoebe sat in her corner of the front seat, not crying, not even sniffling. She clenched a wad of handkerchief in her small hand so fiercely that the knuckles whitened. Holt saw that she was in a worse way than if she'd broken down and had the relief of tears.

At the funeral home, George White acted as go-between with Reg and got the funeral set for Wednesday afternoon. Miss Phoebe sat apart, leaving matters to Holt, as though she did not trust herself to think about the distressing details.

The ride back to the house was the same. Holt feared she'd go to pieces if he so much as tried to console her, much less talk business.

When he took her to the door, he hesitated. Still tautly silent, Miss Phoebe went into the house. Holt stood at the door a moment, puzzled and perturbed.

Then he realized what bothered him. For the first time in the twenty years he could remember, Miss Phoebe hadn't offered some tidbit and a cup of coffee. More than any display of emotion, it brought home to him now how shaken she was.

Relieved that he'd had enough sense to hold his tongue, Holt followed her only as far as the hall, gave her an awkward hug, and then headed for the office.

There was a parking place open in front of Hank Neilson's hardware store. Holt angled his car in, shoved the door open and slid part way out.

Above Neilson's, the gilt letters of the sign, "Holt Lawson, Lawyer", reflected the afternoon sun. Holt realized he had no desire to go up there and sit on his fanny. He wanted to get on with the search for Adelaide's will.

But how? He'd already checked the bank. She'd no doubt

cleaned that box out for fear Townsend could manage to pry into it. The same would go for the bakery and Shelton.

With a muttered, "Nuts!", Holt kicked himself out of the car. From force of habit he took the stairs two at a time, beginning with the first step so he'd miss the squeaky one, and pushed open the door to the big room that doubled as reception room and library.

High old-fashioned ceilings gave the room an airy, spacious appearance. But now, preoccupied with the matter of Adelaide's will, Holt didn't get the feeling of respite, of lowered tension, that the cool, quiet office usually gave him.

Burgess wasn't at her desk. Crossing the reception area, Holt went through the library stacks. Then he came back and looked in his private office.

Still no Burgess. He felt an annoyance that he knew was unreasonable. She hadn't skipped out on any work.

Her typewriter was uncovered, however; her desk in disarray. That meant she'd be back.

Crossing to Burgess's desk, he searched for any sort of mail or message to occupy himself with. The basket where she put these was empty.

But a book lay on the desk, held open with paper weights. Holt glanced down at the poem Burgess had been reading:

> "I love your lips when they're wet with wine
> And red with a wild desire;
> I love your eyes when the lovelight lies
> Lit with a passionate fire."

Now here was something to distract his thoughts! He skimmed on, lingering over the more lush passages.

Just then the squeaky step on the entrance stairway screeched. Holt looked up. Burgess marched in.

Opening his arms, he advanced on her and entreated, " 'Kiss me sweet with your warm wet mouth still fragrant

94

with ruby wine'.''

Burgess took her lower lip between her teeth. She gave a long look first at her book and then at Holt. Several seconds went by. Then she shrugged and said briskly, "My warm wet mouth is fragrant with coffee. Have a cinnamon roll. Bet you missed lunch.''

The danger signals didn't escape Holt. But they made teasing Burgess even more stimulating.

She put the sack she was carrying on her desk and sat down. "Go on. Help yourself to a roll.''

Holt shook his head. He knew he'd be acting like a horse's ass if he pestered Burgess further. But he couldn't help himself. If his frustrations about Adelaide's will hadn't been edging in on him, he'd have behaved.

As it was, he walked behind her, put his arms around her shoulders and recited with feeling, " 'With your body so young and warm in my arms, it sets my poor heart aflame'.''

Burgess got to her feet in a jerky movement and spun away. "I tried to shush you nicely," she snapped. "What does it take? A sledge hammer?''

Even knowing he was off sides, Holt felt ruffled. "Okay,'' he said. "But I don't see why you read stuff that slops over with sentiment if you're going to put the chill on every man who looks at you.''

Burgess moved so that the desk was between them. Then she faced him, arms akimbo, eyes glistening. "Just put it down that I'm cold-blooded," she flared. "Now do you have any office work for me?''

Holt surveyed the young, warm body across the desk. With her hands on her hips and her legs slightly apart, Burgess had her dress stretched against her shapely curves.

Suddenly serious, Holt leaned across the desk top toward her. "Burgess, you aren't cut out to be an old maid, but you're headed that way. You ought to see . . .''

95

Burgess cut him short. "Shut up, damn you, Holt!"

Taken aback, Holt did just that.

Burgess's breasts rose and fell angrily. "Now get this through your thick head," she stormed. "I don't want your amateur analysis. I damned well know why I'm like I am. And I damned well intend to stay that way!"

Holt felt a confusion of emotions. He'd never heard Burgess curse, never had her snatch his head off. It left him surprised and hurt.

Suddenly he felt tired. Lack of sleep and the tensions of the trial and its aftermath were catching up on him. He crossed to the office couch and sat down, resting his head against its back.

"Good Lord, Burgess," he said, "let's us not fight. I've got enough trouble everywhere else."

For a moment she continued to stand there with her hands on her hips. Then she turned and circled her desk.

"Put your feet up and try using the couch arm for a pillow," she said. "It works fine."

He did as she suggested and closed his eyes, giving way to his exhaustion.

The door to his private office clicked open and shut, and water splashed in his washbasin. Then he sensed Burgess coming to his side. She put a cool, damp cloth across his eyes and forehead. It blocked the overhead light from his eyelids and soothed the taut feeling from his brow. But even as he relaxed, he wondered about Burgess and how to make a better start toward a talk with her.

And he began to plan how best to tackle Miss Phoebe, without upsetting her, on the subject of what Adelaide had done with her valuables.

But, before he'd solved either of these tantalizing problems, he sank into a blessed sleep.

Chapter 9

Waking, Holt opened his eyes. Pitch dark concealed his surroundings. For a moment he lay still, trying to figure out where he was.

Touching and squeezing with his fingers, he explored his bed. A firm, narrow, leathery something. Then he remembered. Burgess had got him to nap on the office couch.

No sounds from outside penetrated into the office. Holt pulled himself up, flicked on the lights and looked at his watch. Seven o'clock. Force of habit sent him to check Burgess's basket. A single message lay there.

Holt grabbed for it, hoping against hope that it might be from Miss Phoebe and give him a chance to talk to her.

But the message Burgess had left read, "6:15. Connie called. Won't be by tonight. Cousin Reg and Cousin Connie are going to their cousin's in Tyler."

That suited him. Since he'd ignored Connie's advice and ripped into Adelaide's heir apparent, he'd prefer coming up with a new will before discussing the consequences of his conduct. He glanced down at the message again.

"6:15". So Burgess had stayed long after office hours to keep the phone from waking him. Holt started whistling a cheery little tune.

And that "Cousin Reg . . . Cousin Connie . . . Tyler

cousin." No doubt Connie had emphasized the family relationship; but Burgess, by her exact repetition, made it sound fishy as hell.

Smiling, Holt shook his head. Could it be that the cold-natured Burgess was capable of at least some emotion? Jealousy, for instance?

All at once he realized that he'd sloughed off the day's trials somewhere along the way and now felt refreshed. And hungry. He decided on a steak, home, and an early morning call to Miss Phoebe.

An hour later Holt parked his station wagon in its usual spot by the back porch of his house and got out, being careful not to step on Snubby in the dark.

But no Snubby came charging from the house. Surprised, Holt trotted up the stairs to the back porch.

A piteous whine sounded inside the dark kitchen. Stepping inside, Holt switched on the light.

A heavy-set man sat at the kitchen table. Holt stopped short and blinked in surprise. "What the hell are you doing here?" he demanded.

The dark, coarsely handsome young man braced his left arm on top of the table and used it as a rest for a monstrous revolver that he pointed at Holt's belly. "Mr. Fox wants to talk to you," he said.

A muffled whimper came through his words from across the kitchen. Holt noted that his laundry bag had been slung on the closet door there, and saw something stir inside.

Holt nodded toward the bag. "That my dog?" he demanded.

Fleshy lips parted in a grin that erased the extreme cupid's bow of the intruder's mouth. "He's all right. Tried to make like Rin-tin-tin."

A flush of resentment warmed Holt's face. Grimly he

measured the distance to the kitchen table.

The pistol's enormous muzzle promptly came up. Holt abandoned the idea of charging and reminded himself that Snubby would be getting ample air through the porous sack.

The man at the table stood and stretched. Sizing the intruder up, Holt saw that the width of those shoulders didn't come from any padding in the striped coat.

The young thug gestured with his gun. "Coming in, Mr. Fox," he called.

The lights in the front room flashed on. Holt moved slowly, finding it difficult to march meekly along on command.

"Step on it!" Something hard, — the pistol barrel no doubt, — prodded his spinal column.

Boiling with indignation, Holt gambled that the fellow behind would keep him intact for the talk with Fox. "You've got a hell of a nerve, Junior," he growled, "busting in here . . ."

The pistol barrel glinted. A blow slammed down on Holt's skull. Lights burst and whirled. He dropped to one knee.

The broad-shouldered youth stepped around in front. A mace-like fist drove into Holt's stomach. Groggy, Holt tried to stand. A hard open hand slapped him to the floor. He felt himself lifted and dragged.

Then a far-off voice said, "Here he is, Mr. Fox." Supporting hands were withdrawn.

Holt's knees buckled, and he dropped into a chair. But by shaking his head, he got things to start clearing.

Across the coffee table a slight, swarthy man, thirty-five or thereabouts, sat on the sofa.

"So you're Fox." Holt's voice sounded thick to his own ears.

The man across the table pulled a deck of cards from his

pocket. "You'll come around in a minute," he said. Five stud hands formed almost magically as long slender fingers flicked cards to the table.

Taking deep breaths, Holt tried to steady the choppy, angry gasps that made his chest heave. The swarthy man studied the hands he'd dealt. He had an elongated nose from which forehead and chin retreated. Occasionally he fingered a thin-line moustache.

After a few moments Holt clasped his hands together and hooked them around his knees to stop their shaking. "I've got my wind," he said. "Now what the hell do you want?"

"Forty thousand dollars, to be exact." The gambler scooped up his cards. "The thirty-five thousand Bailey owes me and five for the time it's taking to collect it."

Holt made his shrug apparent and tried a feeler. "That's got nothing to do with me."

"You put it very well." Strong teeth showed in a flashing smile.

Both smile and retort rubbed Holt the wrong way. "You didn't need to come busting in here to tell me that," he flared.

Fox's black eyes turned flinty. "I came here to tell you I don't want any interference from you until I get my money. Kane's filing applications to appoint Bailey administrator and to sell the plant. No matter what you find, you stay away from the court until I'm paid or you'll have a really rough session with Gino."

Holt felt his temper slipping. "Just like that!" he exclaimed. "You're going to handle me just like you do gutless little Reggie!"

Fox gave a short laugh. "Why not? Wasn't that how you came to quit pro ball — when you lost your guts?"

Holt started. So that was the word that had circulated among the smart boys. His stomach began to churn.

A few feet to Fox's left his young muscle man stood, gun in hand, a smirk on his sensual lips. Gauging the line-up against him, Holt debated how to take that gun out of the play.

In a sudden movement Fox leaned across the table, thrusting a scornful, menacing face near Holt's. "Do you need further convincing?"

"You've overlooked one big thing." Holt stood. "But I'm not going to sit here talking while my dog suffocates."

Gino stepped forward, his pistol leveled.

"Wait, Gino," Fox commanded. And then, to Holt: "What have I overlooked, Mr. Lawson?"

Ignoring the query, Holt turned to the young man with the gun and looked him up and down. "Does your mommy know you're out, sonny?" he gibed.

The vulgarly handsome face contorted. The pistol hand whipped up to striking position.

"Gino!" Fox burst out. "Wait!"

The young hoodlum hesitated.

Pivoting, crouching, all in one movement, Holt brushed the pistol aside with his left hand and crashed a roundhouse right against Gino's jaw.

The eyes above the jaw glazed. Letting anger take over, Holt slammed his fists into stomach and face as the heavy body slid to the floor.

The pistol dropped from the gunman's hand. Diving, Holt seized it, then turned on Fox.

"Hold it!" the gambler cried, hands raised, palms out. "I never carry a gun."

An eye still on Fox, Holt stripped the silk necktie from the unconscious Gino, pulled the thick wrists in back and bound them together.

Gino groaned.

Holt picked up the gun again and motioned Fox toward

the kitchen. "Get the laundry bag," he commanded.

Fox moved promptly. A mixture of frantic yelps and menacing snarls started up as, still under Holt's watchful surveillance, he lugged the bag back to the front room.

Holt turned the sack upside down and tumbled Snubby and an assortment of shirts and underwear onto the floor. Suddenly quiet, the little Peke shook loose from the laundry and looked about uncertainly through his popped eyes.

Now Gino stirred. With the laundry bag in one hand, Holt collared the inert thug, dragged him across the room and propped him on the stairway against the banisters.

Gino opened his eyes. Fox's hiss, sudden and unexpected, startled Holt. The gambler spat out something in a foreign tongue. The young hood flinched and paled.

"Save it, Fox." Holt slapped the sack over Gino's head, tightened the draw strings and lashed them to a banister. Then he stood and turned to the gambler. "Now let's talk."

Fox shrugged and returned to the sofa. "You've got the high cards showing. That puts it up to you."

Breathing normally again, Holt crossed to where the gambler sat and took the chair on the opposite side of the coffee table. "You were afraid I'd turn up something that would queer your deal with Reg. What? A later will of Adelaide Bailey's?"

Fox considered. "If I give you the whole story, will you keep the bargain she made?"

"Go ahead."

"She was going to give me forty thousand for Reg Bailey's stock — if I waited till after the trial."

Holt smiled wryly. That would be like Adelaide. But he felt his pulse quicken. Fox spoke as though Holt, not the bank, would be acting for Adelaide.

The lack of any response seemed to upset the gambler. He pulled a sheet of engraved paper from his pocket and slapped it on the table. Holt recognized the stock certificate form of Adelaide's Breads, Inc.

"That's one thousand shares of the bakery corporation," Fox declared. "Reg Bailey's. Signed over to me. What the hell would I have it for if she hadn't promised to buy it?"

Holt moistened his lips and tried to conceal the excitement growing within him. "Why come to me? The executor may hire a different lawyer."

Fox snorted. "In this will, the executor *is* you. Now do you want to know where she stashed it?"

Holt rubbed moist palms along his thighs. "You've got yourself a deal," he agreed.

Fox pulled a pad and gold pen from his inner coat pocket and began to write briskly.

In his mind's eye Holt saw himself sitting in Adelaide's chair at the head of the long, gleaming directors' table. But all such was strictly dealing in futures. Returning to the present, he demanded, "Where's the will?"

"Just a minute now," Fox demurred. "It isn't often I get something that'll stand up in court."

Impatiently Holt watched Fox finish his scribbling. Then the gambler tossed the memorandum he'd drafted across the table.

Holt picked up the piece of paper. In clear, concise language it spelled out a contract for the purchase of Reg's one thousand shares of stock for forty thousand dollars.

Surprised, Holt noted the legal phrases, the exactness of the clause making it contingent upon his appointment as executor. He stared at Fox. "You're a lawyer!"

"I'm a gambler!" Fox gave a short, bitter laugh. "The only clients I ever had came from the welfare department."

For Holt, Fox's background, however unique, held no interest comparable with his own situation. Hastily he jotted his signature at the bottom of the memo and handed it back.

Fox glanced at the paper; nodded. "There's a wall safe in Miss Bailey's bedroom. Behind a picture of Reginald. The will's in the safe."

Holt felt his pulse racing. "You're sure, now?" he insisted.

"When a man owes me money, I *make* sure," Fox declared. He reached for the stock certificate.

Before the gambler's fingers closed on it, Holt snatched up the engraved paper and pocketed it.

"Now wait a minute," Fox protested. "That's not yours until I get my money."

"I know it," Holt agreed. "But I'll keep it for insurance. If you don't have the certificate, you can't sell to somebody else. I want you working with me."

Fox shrugged, but his black eyes smoldered with resentment. "Keep it," he growled. "I've got your contract. And I don't need anything to collect from Bailey if he comes into the dough."

"So stop grousing." Holt grinned. "Either way, you're in good shape."

Abruptly Fox's mood seemed to change. Holt found himself looking into a pair of eyes that mocked him with cynical amusement.

"You're right, counselor," Fox conceded. He stood, folded the memorandum agreement and shoved it into his pocket. "I'm in good shape — maybe better than you. Kane won't tell me why — but he sure acts like he doesn't ever expect to see that will probated."

Chapter 10

Stunned, Holt sat reappraising his situation. That crack about the dubious validity of Adelaide's will had taken the wind out of him more effectively than a kick in the stomach.

Fox jerked his head toward the figure trussed to the banister with the laundry sack. "Any reason I shouldn't turn butterfingers loose and take off?"

His mind absorbed with a vital problem, Holt shook his head. If there was one thing he knew in that moment, it was the imperative necessity of getting Judge Woodruff to put him in charge of Adelaide's affairs pending the outcome of any contest on her will.

If Reg stepped into Adelaide's shoes, he'd fire Holt and take away the retainers from the bank and bakery. Holt's law office would close before the will contest could be called up for trial.

That grim prospect drove him to said office the next morning long before usual hours. The door at the foot of the stairs was already open. Surprised, Holt took the steps in his usual two-at-a-time run and shoved the upper door open.

Burgess swiveled around in her chair, her dark brown eyes wide with surprise. An open file lay on her desk.

Holt nodded toward it. "What got you here so early?"

"I can tell there's trouble brewing, and I don't want to

miss anything." Eyes sparkling, she turned back to her desk. "Thought I'd see if we'd stuck anything in Adelaide's folder that would give us a clue to her will."

"Reg's gambler friend dropped in on me last night. He says there's a will in Adelaide's home safe."

"If she had a will that Reg knew about, you'd know about it, too."

Holt smiled wryly. "Not necessarily. If it puts me in charge, she might have given Reg the bad news while she held back on the good. What worries me — if she didn't go to Dad, she must have written it herself. There're a dozen ways she could have botched it."

"Not Adelaide!" Burgess shook her head firmly. A lock of black hair fell down, and she brushed it back.

Holt started for the library stacks, hesitated. "Burgess, you better put a note on the door that we'll be closed today. And I don't think there's any need of your coming back after the funeral."

Burgess nodded and reached for a sheet of paper. Continuing to the stacks, Holt thumbed the form until he located a model for an application to be appointed temporary administrator of a decedent's estate.

Burgess came back from her errand, smoothed the skirt of her navy blue dress and gave Holt an inquiring look.

"Grab your book," Holt said. "I am about to dictate what we should call a petition to keep the wolf from the door."

Pacing back and forth in front of Burgess' desk, Holt dictated his application, setting forth his familiarity with Adelaide's affairs, her naming of him as executor in her will, the necessity of having her stock voted at shareholders' meetings, and concluding with the fervent prayer that Woodruff appoint him temporary administrator of her estate.

"By the way," Burgess asked, "will they still have the

shareholders' meeting of Adelaide's Breads Friday? We haven't done anything on it."

"When you finish this, you might as well type up the usual resolutions. Just leave the dates blank. I'll check with Shelton."

"How soon do you want this?"

Holt made a wry face. "I may never want it if I don't turn up a valid will naming me executor. Without that, I'd be just a buttinsky."

"And when you do find the will, you'll want me to have finished this yesterday." Burgess smiled. "I'll get started."

Having gotten his application into production, Holt crossed back to the library area and wheeled in behind the first stack.

The tall black volumes of Vernon's Annotated Statutes occupied several shelves. Holt pulled down the title, "Probate Code", and pored over the sections that set forth the requirements for the preparation, execution and proof of a will.

The annotator seemed to have taken an especial delight in collecting cases in which do-it-yourself testators had stubbed their toes. As he read, Holt imagined each one applying to Adelaide's will.

John Doe had failed to recite faithfully the magic words required for that legal sorcery, "execution in due form". Feeling suddenly warm, Holt loosened his tie.

Mary Roe had written and signed what would have been a perfectly good will — had she not typed a part of it and then failed to get the two witnesses required for a will not one hundred percent in her handwriting.

Testator Y executed his will at the corner filling station as he left on what was to be his last vacation. It never entered his head that the strapping youth he had sign as a witness was under fourteen and disqualified.

Holt snapped the volume shut. If he didn't divert himself, he was going to shock Miss Phoebe by irreverently rifling the dead woman's bedroom even before Adelaide had had a decent burial.

From the other side of the stack came the steady pounding of typewriter keys. Holt put his eye to the space on the shelf where the volume, "Probate Code", had stood. Through the slot he could see Burgess going hammer and tongs at the task of typing the application.

Now, completely engrossed, she stretched her long, shapely legs out in front of her. Holt felt a smile titillate the corners of his mouth. He knew what was coming next.

Never pausing in her typing, Burgess caught the heel of her left shoe in the crook of the right and pulled it off. Next the left foot went to work on her right shoe and gradually removed it. Holt chuckled softly.

Now Burgess pinned the toe of her left stocking to the floor with her right heel and pulled her leg back, loosening the tight-fitting nylon. Then she repeated the process with her other leg. A happy little sigh escaped her. She pulled her legs back under the desk and jiggled them briskly. Throughout the entire proceding her typing never slackened — and now the tempo quickened.

Watching her made Holt think of the way Snubby instinctively sought his simple creature comforts. Burgess was a healthy young animal, too. Surely deep down she had basic drives: — to mate, to bring forth young and care for them.

A sudden, sharp buzz sounded at Burgess's desk. Holt snapped out of his musing and stuck "Probate Code" back in its place. The buzz resumed. Rounding the stack, Holt saw Burgess pick up the telephone.

She listened a moment, then looked up. "It's Judge Woodruff for you," she said.

Holt couldn't imagine any good tidings that might have

occasioned his honor's call. Going into his private office, he sat uneasily on the edge of his deak and put the receiver to his ear.

Judge Woodruff actually sounded uncomfortable. "Holt, I know Adelaide's funeral is this afternoon, but Kane's out in the courtroom with an application he insists I act on."

Holt felt a warning tingle. "What kind of application?" he asked.

"He wants me to appoint Reginald temporary administrator of his aunt's estate. Says there's a stockholders' meeting coming up Friday that makes it necessary."

Holt doubled the telephone cord and whipped it against his thigh. "I haven't received any notice, Judge," he protested. "Haven't even seen a copy of his petition."

"I can make the appointment without notice where there's an urgency. Only reason I called you is to be sure I have all the facts. I think I ought to authorize Bailey to vote the stock if it's going to be his to do as he pleases with ultimately."

"It isn't," Holt said shortly. "Judge, give me until tomorrow, and I'll bring you Adelaide's last will."

"Very well. Nine o'clock."

Holt considered. Suppose he hit a snag getting into the safe? "Give me until afternoon, Judge," he urged. "The stockholders' meeting isn't until Friday."

"I'll make it two o'clock," Judge Woodruff said firmly. "I think they're entitled to an answer by then."

As soon as the judge hung up, Holt dialed Connie's number.

Connie answered herself with a sleepy, "Hello."

"Wake up," Holt said. "I want to ask you something."

"I was about to call you. Reg ordered a family car for the funeral. Don't you think you ought to go with us? In spite of . . ." Connie left it there.

Holt had no desire to ride with Reg, but he didn't want to make Miss Phoebe feel excluded. "I promised to take Miss Phoebe. If . . ."

"Reg wouldn't want that. He says Miss Phoebe put Adelaide up to a lot of her little games, especially with him."

"Nuts. Count me out." Holt scribbled a note to remind himself to call for a limousine for Miss Phoebe and himself.

A pause, on Connie's part. Then, "You said you wanted to ask me something, Holt."

"I do." Holt tried to keep the irritation out of his voice, but Connie hadn't even had to debate which car she belonged in. "You were buddying around with Reg last night. Did he say anything about another will of Adelaide's?"

"Well . . ." Connie hesitated. "We weren't talking much about . . ."

"Come off it, Connie," Holt said shortly. "You'd both be full of it. Kane's asked Woodruff to name Reg administrator and order the plant sold. What gives Reg the idea her will's no good?"

"I don't know! I don't know!"

Holt heard her draw in a long shaky breath, then begin to sob. In a moment the sobbing stopped.

"Listen, Holt. I honestly don't know. But it doesn't make any difference. You've *got* to let the sale go through. Dad is nearly out of his mind. You just don't . . ."

"Hold it, Connie," Holt said sharply. "Get a grip on yourself. I've told your father I'll work things out for him. But I'm not going to see my biggest client sold and let all our plans go down the drain just because he's come unglued."

Not until she and Holt were back in the funeral home's limousine and being driven away from the cemetery did Miss Phoebe take out her handkerchief and let loose with some tears. For Holt, her acknowledgment and acceptance, at last,

110

of her grief came as a relief. He felt his own breathing ease.

But Miss Phoebe wept for only a moment. Watching carefully for any signs of her getting wound up into the same state of tension as she'd been in the day before, Holt saw something he'd never noticed before.

A very firm little chin poked out of Miss Phoebe's round, kindly face. Miss Phoebe wasn't about to go to pieces. Miss Phoebe was mad!

He waited until they got to Adelaide's house and settled in their usual seats at the round white table in the kitchen. Then he asked, "What is it, Miss Phoebe?"

"That boy knows Adelaide said I was to live out my days here." She jerked on the burner beneath the coffee pot and snatched up an apron. "I said why didn't he move back and take her room. And right at her grave he says that'll be fine and he won't need a housekeeper."

Holt felt his nerves draw taut. Reg was damned sure of matters if he'd ordered Miss Phoebe out!

Yanking the apron around her dumpy waist, Miss Phoebe knotted it.

The very thought of downing any food or drink sent a flutter through Holt's stomach. He stood. "Can you open the safe in Adelaide's bedroom?"

Miss Phoebe nodded. "She showed me. Said somebody besides her ought to know. But everything important's at the bank."

Holt crossed to the stove and turned down the burner under the coffee. "Let's go see," he said.

Adelaide had operated true to form. Reg knew where the will was but not how to get into the safe. Miss Phoebe could open the safe but didn't know anything was there. And Holt, presumably named to handle her affairs, Adelaide had kept in the dark about all of it.

Miss Phoebe plodded slowly up the stairs. Holt put his

hands under her arms and helped, hurried, fairly lifted her up the stairs.

In the high-ceilinged room that had been Adelaide's the late afternoon sun poured through the French windows throwing ample light on the wall where Reg's picture hung.

Holt removed the picture. A steel door with a combination lock stood exposed. Gesturing for Miss Phoebe to have at it, Holt stepped back and squatted on the edge of the nearest piece of furniture, Adelaide's four-poster bed.

Miss Phoebe shuffled up to the safe and stared uncertainly at the dial.

Holt tensed. "Don't you have the combination written down?" he asked.

"Adelaide wouldn't let me," Miss Phoebe complained. "But I've worked it."

She began to spin the dial to the left, hesitated, then started the first, clearing spin to the right.

Holt gripped the side of the mattress he sat on and squeezed until the pressure hurt his fingertips.

Miss Phoebe finished a series of turns, tried the handle. It didn't budge. She began to cry, started another set of spins, stopping now and then to clear her eyes with her apron.

"Adelaide used to forget things, too." Miss Phoebe's voice quivered.

Holt gave her shoulders a reassuring squeeze as he slipped from the room. Using the downstairs phone he dialed the number of Neilson's Hardware Store.

Mrs. Neilson sounded harassed. "Hank's at the lake fishing. Our busiest afternoon. Won't be home till dark."

Back upstairs, Holt peeked into the bedroom. Miss Phoebe was still fumbling with the dial. Aware of a mounting uneasiness, he ran down the stairs again and called Burgess's house. Burgess's mother reported her not at home.

Frustrated, Holt drew a long breath. With no real hope,

he dialed his office number.

The soft burr-r-ring sound of the ringing signal repeated several times, then Burgess answered briskly, "Mr. Lawson's office."

"Thank the Lord!" Holt exclaimed. "Burgess, how about getting your ski rig out and tracking down Hank Neilson? He's fishing, and I need him."

"Running into problems with the safe?"

"I've run into a stone wall so far, and I've got to have that will for Woodruff tomorrow. If you'll get Neilson, I'll keep trying here."

"I'm on my way!"

Holt returned to the bedroom. He found Miss Phoebe sitting on the side of the bed, her shoulders slumped. She started up.

He waved her back. "You rest a while," he said. "I'll go through Adelaide's desk and see if I can find anything that looks like a memorandum of the combination."

Miss Phoebe sank back on the bed. "I'm sure it'll come to me," she said weakly.

Holt advanced on Adelaide's quaint, bird's-eye maple desk and opened it. Every compartment and drawer bulged with her notes. Fully aware of the hopelessness of sorting through that mass of scribblings in time, he nevertheless made a start, cursing the clumsiness of his trembling fingers.

At last the front door bell rang. Holt gestured for Miss Phoebe to sit tight and raced down the stairs.

Hank Neilson was wearing soiled khaki pants and a slightly damp khaki shirt. "Burgess rode my tail till she got me here," he declared. "Said she was going back to the office to finish something."

"I sure appreciate your giving up your fishing afternoon." Holt led the way to the bedroom and pointed.

Neilson advanced on the safe, ran his fingers across the

smooth, polished steel front and spun the high-wrought combination dial.

"Boy, what a beauty," he breathed.

Holt glared at the object of Neilson's admiration. "Can you open it?" he demanded.

"Of course not." Neilson patted the metal face. "No run-of-the-mill locksmith could touch that baby."

"Then use a blowtorch!" Holt exploded. "Just get it open!"

Neilson shook his head. "What's inside might go up in smoke."

Holt put a hand on Neilson's shoulder. Taking a couple of long breaths, he tried to steady his voice. "Hank, I've *got* to get what's in that safe by in the morning. Now tell me what to do."

"Let me make a long-distance call."

Holt led Neilson to the bedroom telephone. The locksmith placed a call to Dallas. Hardly able to contain himself, Holt endured interminable bantering and good-natured argument in which Neilson was not nearly firm enough.

Finally Neilson hung up.

"How'd you make out?" Holt searched Neilson's face for some indication. "I couldn't tell from this end of the conversation."

"Well, he can't come down here. He's catching a plane for Los Angeles in the morning."

A leaden weight seemed to settle in Holt's chest.

"But he said if you'd get it there not a minute later than eight in the morning, he'd work on it. That is, if it's all right to chip it out and burn it free."

Holt made a quick calculation and nodded. When he scorched the highway, he could make Dallas in two hours.

Miss Phoebe came forward at her slow gait. "Holt," she

114

protested, "that'd ruin the wall. I'm sure I'll remember how to open it tomorrow."

Unable to endure more, Holt took her by the shoulders and led her back to the bed. "Miss Phoebe," he counseled cruelly, "don't worry about one wall when Reg is trying to throw you out of the whole house."

Miss Phoebe's eyes went wide. As for Hank Neilson, his reaction was pure disaster, "Say," he exclaimed, "come to think of it, I can't go ripping into this wall without Reg Bailey's okay."

Holt's patience snapped. It would be tomorrow before an order could be had from Woodruff.

Without an order, he'd be a common trespasser, an out and out safecracker, and in contempt of court.

Throwing caution to the winds, he marched over to Neilson.

The hardware man fell back a step.

"Hank," Holt grated, "Adelaide's will puts me in charge of her estate. Unless you want to lose that fat account out at the plant, you get started chipping!"

Chapter 11

At daybreak Thursday morning, Holt eased his station wagon over the dip in the road entering the Dallas highway. The rear end springs collapsed, sounding a protesting wh-a-ang.

Holt muttered a "damn" and looked back to see that Adelaide's safe was riding okay.

At every uneven spot in the road, the back end sounded as though something would give. Holt weighed the time it would take to get a truck and transfer his load, decided it would be faster to go on.

Moments later another unexpected bump crashed the car's body against the axle. Holt realized that continued speed was going to leave him stranded on the side of the road while the expert on safes winged his way to California and Woodruff pounded his gavel for the two o'clock hearing.

But ahead miles and miles of highway stretched out with Dallas an impossible distance away. Sweat started under Holt's arms; but he made himself crawl along, straining his eyes for rough spots in the road.

Eight o'clock passed. Already he was late. His leg ached with the strain of gingerly speeding, slowing, speeding again.

Nine o'clock. Breathing hard, Holt piloted his load cautiously through city traffic.

117

Nine-thirty. Holt pulled into a loading zone at the address Neilson had given him. The sign over the open door read, "Calhoun's: Safes, Magic Supplies".

Grateful that he'd made it, Holt hurried into the shop; then stopped short, taken aback. A center aisle divided the small building, and the two parts of the shop had as unlikely a connection as would Cinderella hooked up as a Siamese twin to one of her sisters.

On the left, heavy black shelves and stout, unlighted display counters held up to view a supply of sturdy locks and safes. But on the right, concealed lights in ceiling, counters, and shelves beckoned the eye to a display of conjuring equipment.

Recovering from his momentary surprise, Holt looked around for the man Neilson had called.

A tall, lanky individual behind the magic display counter was unrolling across its top a piece of green billiard table cloth. A youngster of about eleven faced him, eyes sparkling with anticipation.

Holt hustled over to the counter. "Mr. Calhoun?" he asked.

Friendly brown eyes looked up from beneath active black brows. "You must be Mr. Lawson."

Holt nodded. "I've got the safe outside."

The tall man finished smoothing the cloth, wiped his hands on the quaint neck-high blue apron he wore, and took a pea and three shells from a pasteboard box.

"Sorry you couldn't make it here sooner," he said. "I've got to leave for the airport soon as my helper comes in. But quick as I finish with this young man, I'll take a look at your safe and try to suggest somebody."

Holt chewed on his lower lip. From what Neilson had said, he wouldn't find anyone else soon enough to be back in Woodruff's court at two with Adelaide's will. He began to appraise the man behind the counter.

The pale hollowness of Calhoun's cheeks exaggerated the large homely nose, the strong chin, and the heavy sideburns. A certain familiarity about the man puzzled Holt. Then all at once he had it.

Calhoun could have stepped out of the insurance company's calendar that hung in the County Clerk's office. He'd made himself up as young Abe Lincoln, the storekeeper. And now Holt could guess that Calhoun's trip was to Hollywood.

The deduction didn't seem useful. Holt had no Hollywood connections with which to establish a rapport. He scouted along the counter toward the back of the shop.

On the shelf beneath the glass was an amazing display of mystifying effects: a box that would make a coin vanish, a vase in which a ball would appear or disappear, an enchanted bottle that only its owner could make lie on its side.

Holt noted that the more expensive tricks were toward the rear of the shop. Here were beautiful silks guaranteed to change color, tie and untie themselves, separate into a myriad of tiny handkerchiefs or blend into one large vari-colored silk.

Still he'd found no opener for a try at ingratiating himself with Calhoun.

On the locksmith side of the back wall hung some snapshots of Calhoun holding up a string of bass. Pine trees stood in the background.

Holt turned quickly. "Do you go to East Texas often?"

Calhoun was engaged in weaving his shells in a serpentine pattern. "I come from East Texas," he said. "Jefferson."

Jefferson! Holt drew in a sharp breath. The perfect case in point of the fate that impended for Pinewood!

Once Jefferson had been the proud metropolis of east Texas. Now its century-old mansions stood rotting except for

119

the few bought and restored by city-rich looking for instant gentility. An angry Jay Gould had promised it when he scrawled "End of Jefferson, Texas" on the Excelsior Hotel register — and had brought it about by taking his railroad elsewhere.

"Come on over," Calhoun called. "You'll never learn the shell game any cheaper."

Holt moved promptly to demonstrate his interest in anything Calhoun might be doing. But he fixed his eyes on the homely face and tried to guess whether this man would resent or rejoice at Pinewood's suffering Jefferson's lot.

Calhoun paused and looked up. "Are you watching?" he demanded.

Holt nodded, made himself pay polite attention.

Now Calhoun brushed two of the shells aside as though to eliminate the devices for misdirection. Performing in slow motion, he took the remaining shell and covered the pea with it . . . began moving it about on the cloth-covered counter in a serpentine pattern like a carnival bunco artist.

As he pushed the shell away from him, however, he raised the edge nearest his hand to allow the pea to escape into the vise of his thumb and second finger.

Even as slowly as Calhoun did the trick Holt almost missed the subtle sleight of hand. And now he couldn't see the pea, concealed as it was under Calhoun's forefinger.

Calhoun lifted the shell. "No pea!" he chuckled. "Now if you see your sucker's suspicious, grab an empty shell, pull it to you, and let the pea slip back under."

His strong fingers moved swiftly, as he spoke. Lifting the shell, he revealed the pea resting on the cloth as though it had never moved.

Holt blinked and shook his head, hardly believing the simplicity of the hoax.

Calhoun and his young customer completed their

business. Then, rolling up his green cloth, the magic dealer turned to Holt. "Let's see how tough your safe looks."

Simultaneously, a man entered the shop and walked to the rear. Holt had no doubt it was the helper and that now Calhoun would be restless to take off.

"I'll give you some names," Calhoun said. "You'll have to call them yourself."

"You don't need to look at the safe," Holt asserted. "It's tough. You got any idea I can track down somebody, get it opened, and be back in Pinewood by two?"

Calhoun gave Holt a level look. "If you need a top man, I'd say you'd be lucky to get your box cracked by next week."

Holt gripped the counter, hard. He felt his veneer of civilized behavior cracking. Desperately he hung on, trying for a few more moments of self control.

"I've got to be back in Pinewood by two. *With* what's in that safe — or the business that keeps Pinewood going will be sold and it'll be as dead a burg as Jefferson."

"That's your problem," Calhoun declared. He wiped his hands nervously on his apron and pushed at his rolled sleeves. "My agent's made a contract."

Holt fished a piece of paper out of his pocket, unscrewed his pen with trembling fingers, thrust pen and paper across the counter.

"Here," he blazed. "Write it. 'End of Pinewood, Texas.' We'll hang it on the courthouse wall and remember you just like Jefferson does Jay Gould!"

Calhoun's hands stopped as if abruptly frozen solid. The corners of his mouth drew down in a bitter arc. "That bastard! It bankrupt my family when he bypassed the city with his railway. Why the hell they've got his private car in the park instead of burning it, I don't know."

"So why do you want to pull the same kind of trick on

121

Pinewood?"

The searching look that Calhoun gave Holt then seemed to come from deep within his dark brown eyes. It lasted a long, trying time. Finally he turned on his heel and brushed through the canvas curtain that screened the rear of the shop.

All at once Holt realized he'd reached the end of his endurance. He'd sat on himself until Adelaide was buried, walked on eggs with Miss Phoebe, spent the last five hours nursing the damned car springs. He'd had it!

Calhoun was *not* going to walk out on him until he'd opened that damned safe!

Doubling his fists, Holt started for the rear of the shop.

But just then Calhoun pushed back through the curtain, wheeling a dolly before him.

He grinned. "Me as Jay Gould would be rotten casting," he said. "Let's go get your safe."

Holt manhandled the dolly and safe from the car into the shop. Preceding him, Calhoun held aside the curtain and nodded toward the rear of the store. Holt trundled his safe on through.

"Careful!" Calhoun barked.

Holt hauled back on the dolly, narrowly missing a triple-mirrored dressing table covered with make-up jars. Eight-by-eleven gloss prints covered the wall from floor to ceiling. Holt blinked his eyes in surprise.

"This way," Calhoun said.

Holt got the dolly in motion again and wheeled it past a rack of theatrical costumes ranging from sackcloth tatters to robes of royal purple.

Calhoun indicated a semi-screened work bench in the corner. Holt, the helper and Calhoun wrestled the safe onto the work bench.

Turning to the helper, Calhoun instructed, "See if they'll

122

yank Oliver off the set for a long-distance call. If he can cover up for me at the conference, I could be there tomorrow for the shooting."

"I sure as hell appreciate this," Holt said. "I hope I can afford to pay anything it costs you."

"Oliver will manage." Calhoun chuckled. "We're identical twins. Once we had both of us on the payroll at two different studios."

Holt eyed the assortment of tools hanging above the work bench.

Calhoun became immediately serious. "If you'll go look around outside, I'll get started," he said. "I can't work with anyone watching."

Holt stepped out swiftly. Calhoun dropped a flimsy curtain across the aperture. Crossing to the wall with the pictures, Holt wondered about the safe expert's professed inability to work in front of a spectator.

The gloss prints showed Calhoun appearing in everything from Shakespeare to burlesque blackout. Holt smiled. It was all too obvious that an audience of one wouldn't bother the seasoned trouper. But exposing his secret working methods would.

Reassuring sounds of beginning activity came from behind the curtain. Then Calhoun called out, "If you're taking in the picture gallery, you can't tell Oliver from me. We used to take some parts as twins. Nowadays, one of us minds the store while the other hams it up. It lets us eat more regularly."

"So when I walked in, you were about to play hookey," Holt observed.

The laugh that came from behind the screen sounded like a small boy busy with a delicious prank. "You had that working for you," Calhoun said, "but you still played a great heavy."

Holt, too, chuckled; then prowled the room. But the costumes occupied him only briefly, and Calhoun offered no further conversation.

Holt flung himself into a chair. Only with difficulty did he resist the urge to ask for a progress report.

"Damn!" The exclamation came from the direction of the work bench.

Holt tensed. "Anything I can do to help?"

Calhoun didn't answer. Holt chewed his lower lip and kept quiet. The small hand on his wrist watch moved toward eleven. He could, he comforted himself, make Pinewood in two hours — *if* he didn't hit a radar trap or have a flat or get stuck behind a truck on the long, hilly no-passing stretches.

Not a sound from behind the curtain. Calhoun must be stuck. Holt quit the hard chair and tried to make himself inspect the conjuring equipment in the front room.

On a magician's table in the corner, a set of Chinese Linking Rings was displayed. Holt drummed his fingers on the table, eyed the mystifying rings without interest and returned to the back room.

The hour hand on his watch passed eleven. Holt counseled himself to stay quiet and in the same instant blurted, "It's after eleven!"

"I know what time it is," Calhoun snapped, all merriment gone from his voice. "Best way for you to help is to shut up."

Holt felt his heart pounding as if he'd been running. He went to his car and reassured himself that the gauge registered ample gas for the trip to Pinewood.

A Dallas city map lay on the seat. He checked and double-checked the shortest route to the highway.

Now all he could do was wait on Calhoun.

Eleven thirty. Returning to the shop, he settled in the chair in the back room. The place had become warmly stuffy.

Eleven forty-five. Holt squirmed helplessly. Sweat trickled from his armpits down his ribs.

Suddenly the flimsy curtain was flung back. "Got it!" Calhoun shouted. "Last tumbler just fell!"

Holt grabbed his briefcase and ran for the work bench.

The locksmith waved a hand at the safe. Holt wrenched the door open and began tumbling little coin purses and jewel boxes into his briefcase.

An elastic band held together a thick stack of folded papers. Holt pawed through the pile until he found a paper on the back of which Adelaide had written the single word, "Will".

Extracting that document, he dumped everything else into his case. The will had no blue back, and no legal secretary would have owned up to its typing.

But, flipping the pages quickly, Holt recognized the language as identical to Adelaide's original will — except that his own name appeared where formerly his father had been named as executor and trustee.

On the last page, Adelaide had written her name firmly. A Thomas Davenport and Bruce Jennings had signed as witnesses. Holt sucked in a lung full of air. Adelaide's will was in proper order! Undamaged! Unrevoked!

All he'd need to prove it up would be the testimony of Davenport or Jennings that Adelaide was old enough, smart enough and had in fact executed the will.

Then he could sit back and let Kane do his damnedest to try to prove Adelaide incompetent at the very time she was actively running Pinewood's largest enterprises!

Burgess ought to get started tracking down the witnesses right away. But where?

The attestation clause recited that the will had been executed in Hilma, Texas. Adelaide must have gotten around to this bit of business while on one of her West Texas

125

vacations.

But what connection had she had with these men? Holt had never heard of either of them.

If there was one thing he knew instantly, it was that he better get hold of these witnesses and nail down their testimony before Kane got to them. And Kane would see the will at two o'clock!

Turning to Calhoun, Holt asked, "Is it all right to make a call if I charge it to my number?"

Calhoun nodded. "There's a phone hanging on the side of the bench there."

Holt got a long distance operator, "I want to talk to a lawyer, Brad . . . Bradford Oates, in Hilma, Texas. Can you rush it please?"

The operator started the usual questions. Holt cut her off. "No, I don't have the area code, I don't have the number, and I don't have but about two minutes time!"

After long moments the operator announced she had Mr. Oates on the line.

"Hi, Brad," Holt said. "This is Holt Lawson."

"Greetings, valiant teammate," Brad's cheery voice boomed. "Practicing law or gone to making a living?"

"I'll be out there tomorrow or next day and we can visit then." Holt let his business-like tone cut off the customary small talk. "Got time to handle a little matter for me?"

"Of course." Brad's tone became crisply business-like also. "What can I do for you?"

"Line up a couple of men who witnessed a woman's will there several years ago. Thomas Davenport and Bruce Jennings. The woman was Adelaide Bailey."

"Where do I find them?"

"That's why I'm calling you," Holt said sharply. "I want statements from them — you know, get them committed that she was sane, signed in their presence, declared it her will,

126

asked them to witness — all that. The usual proof of will."

"Was your gal staying at the hotel?" Brad asked.

"Yes. Why?" Holt felt the beginning of a warning tingle.

"That gives me a starting point. I'll check the register. If they didn't stay there, I'll start on the other tourist traps."

A foreboding of bad news settled like a weight in Holt's chest.

"Brad," he demanded, "Are you sure neither of these men come from Hilma?"

"Not a chance." Brad's tone was positive. "I've politicked every wide place in the road in this county. You won't find a Tom Davenport or Bruce Jennings out here!"

Chapter 12

At 2:15 Thursday afternoon, Holt marched into Judge Woodruff's courtroom with his briefcase in his hand, a speeding ticket in his pocket, and a burn under his collar.

Shelton and Townsend had both parked themselves on the same side of the counsel table with Reg and Kane, lending the open backing of men who could make delivery on both campaign funds and votes.

Circling to the table's unoccupied side, Holt thanked his stars that he had come armed with Adelaide's will and the judge wouldn't be faced with a close decision.

Woodruff glared through his cold, colorless left eye. "I guess we can get started now," he rasped. "Mr. Lawson has finally decided to honor us with his presence."

Holt gave the clock on the back wall an apologetic glance. Just below it, in the middle of the last row of seats, Connie was settling herself. Noting the neutrality of her position, Holt realized that she was still torn by the fear that he couldn't block the sale of Adelaide's plant and still get her father off the hook.

Connie's attention was on arranging her jacket and purse. Holt turned quickly toward the bench so he wouldn't receive any pleading glances she might send.

Across the table Matthew Kane gathered himself and

started up. As always when he faced this opponent, Holt sensed the man's animal energy and cunning; and he felt a bristling at the back of his neck as his own natural instincts roused.

Kane filled his lungs with air and started off in a resonant tone. "Your Honor, since our application was filed first . . ."

Judge Woodruff hastily held up a hand. "Now wait a minute, Matthew. Let's be informal. There isn't any jury to work on, and speeches won't influence me."

Holt nodded agreement. If judges liked to kid themselves that they decided cases solely on the law and the facts, he'd go along. Anyway, he definitely agreed on turning down Kane's volume.

The judge gestured with a couple of blue backed papers. "I've read both these applications, and I think we can save time. If Reginald Bailey is inheriting his aunt's estate outright, I'm not going to knock him out of selling the plant. But if Adelaide Bailey left a will, its provisions control."

"She did just that, Judge!" Holt grabbed Adelaide's will, marched to the bench and handed it over. "Her property goes into a trust. Reg can't gamble it away. Her employees won't lose their jobs."

Woodruff held the will before him and, scowling with concentration, went over it page by page. Holt wondered if the bit about the men's jobs had hit home with the crusty old codger.

The judge finished reading and folded the will.

Kane went forward at once. "May I look at that will, Judge?" he asked.

Woodruff passed the paper down. "It looks in order to me," he commented.

Holt let his body relax against the back of his chair. The will had stood up under its first test.

Kane walked back to his place, examining the instrument

as he went. Then he sat down and scrutinized it page by page.

Holt tensed, readied himself. Kane *had* to try to discredit this will. And the most obvious ground for attack was going to put Holt on the spot.

Kane closed in swiftly. "May I ask where this instrument is supposed to have come from?" His tone sneered at the paper's claim to being a testamentary act.

"I got it from Adelaide's home safe," Holt said. "Your client knew it was there."

Reg looked up with a sort of simper and a raised eyebrow that seemed to say "Who? Me?"

Holt moistened his lips. He already knew where Kane would hit next.

"You mean you broke into decedent's safe without authorization from Judge Woodruff?" Kane demanded.

The judge leaned forward in his chair and frowned. Kane knew the old boy's prejudices. Woodruff was a stickler for legal technicalities jealous of the authority of his court.

Holt gave Kane as casual a look as he could manage. When he spoke, he carefully controlled the tone of his voice, kept the anxiety out, even tried for a little cockiness.

"If you'll read the judge's order authorizing us to search the bank box for a will, you might find its language was broad enough to let me keep on looking."

Never having had any reason to read the routine order in the first place, Holt wondered now if there might not be some truth in his confident statement. Anyway, he smirked and tried to act as though he wanted Kane to pursue the matter further.

Kane seemed to decide Holt was baiting him into a line of attack that would backfire. He shrugged off further discussion of the matter and returned to examining the will. Judge Woodruff leaned back in his chair. Holt squeezed the wood arm of his chair and sucked in a deep breath.

131

Then Kane took the will back to the bench and handed it to the judge. "Notice the bad typing. And no identification of a lawyer preparing it."

Holt went forward and stood opposite Kane. "I don't think it was prepared in a law office . . ." he began.

"Or else it was prepared in a law office to look like it wasn't," Kane snapped.

Holt whirled. "What's that supposed to mean?" he demanded.

"I mean it's a forgery!" Kane retorted.

Holt took a step toward his adversary, bristling with anger.

Cra-a-ack! Woodruff hit his gavel on the desk with a blow that hurt the ear drums.

The rap brought Holt back to proper awareness of time, place, and circumstances. He halted.

The judge gripped the head of his gavel and pointed with its handle. "Now you two *gentlemen* get back where you've got a table between you for the rest of this hearing and address your remarks to the bench and not to each other. *Is that clear?*"

Turning on his heel, Holt went back to his chair. His temper had cooled as quickly as it had flared. Because he'd begun to plan how to cut the ground from under Kane's feet.

Across the table, Kane pointed a finger toward the paper on the judge's bench. "Holt's pulled a cute dodge here. Suppose he uses that to trick you into appointing him temporary administrator. A year from now he can shrug his shoulders and say, 'I didn't write the will. I can't find the witnesses. But I'm entitled to a fat fee for my year's work.' What could anybody do about it?"

"That won't hold water, Judge." Holt felt a pleasant tingle as he set about knocking the bottom out of Kane's argument. "Adelaide told Reg she'd made that will, and he's

132

said as much to too many people. Mr. Townsend, for one."

Townsend looked at Reg and shook his head. Reg shrugged his shoulders. They smiled at each other.

Holt felt a flush in his face. If they were going to make him drag Connie into it, so be it. He turned to the rear of the courtroom and raised his arm.

The back seat was empty! The door into the hall was just ceasing to swing. Holt dropped his arm slowly and turned back to the bench.

Woodruff was looking out over the heads of the men at the counsel table. Neither his friendly right eye nor his repellent walleye hinted at his attitude toward the parties before him.

As things stood, Holt didn't want to chance whom Woodruff might put in charge of Adelaide's affairs. He took a half step forward.

The judge brought his eyes down from the rear wall and focused with the right one.

"Set a definite hearing ten days from now when notice will have run," Holt challenged. "I'll bring in witnesses to prove this will's genuine or you can appoint Reg administrator."

"No!" Kane slammed the heel of his hand on the table and stood, his tremendous frame hunched forward as though he could physically thrust his point upon the court. "A postponement amounts to a ruling against my client. He'll lose the chance to sell. The offer expires unless the shareholders act on it favorably tomorrow."

Instinctively Holt turned toward Shelton and waited for Kane's "That's right, isn't it, Sam?"

But Kane didn't ask Shelton for confirmation.

Wondering, Holt cautioned himself against an automatic distrust of anyone as slick looking as Shelton appeared with his glossy hair, polished nails and resplendent silk suit.

133

Frowning, Shelton looked up at Kane, opened his mouth, hesitated, took his lower lip between his teeth.

Holt felt the quickening pulse, the combined exhilaration and apprehension of a man turning up a card at stud poker.

"Sam," he demanded, "suppose we put off our shareholders' meeting until a week from Monday? Wouldn't your buyers hold the offer on the bakery open until then?"

Shelton started, looked uncomfortably from Kane to Townsend. Judge Woodruff leaned across the judge's desk and cupped his hand to his ear.

Then Shelton squared himself in his chair. "I originally thought we'd *have* to wait until then and told them so. The offer *is* open."

Holt drew a sigh of relief. Woodruff turned his colorless iris on Kane.

"There's one other thing, Judge." Holt hastened to try for a knockout blow while Kane was getting the evil eye. "Adelaide's will says Miss Phoebe can live out her days in the home. If you do postpone this hearing, will you enter some sort of order? Reg has told her to get out."

"That's a lie!" The heel of Kane's hand slammed the heavy table. He turned to Reginald Bailey, but that young man had dropped his eyes to the floor.

For a second Kane looked as though he might turn his hatchet-like hand on his client. Then he seemed to recover himself and faced the bench.

"I assure your honor this wasn't on advice of counsel. I can control my client. I'll see Miss Phoebe isn't turned out. The order appointing Reginald can be drawn to prevent it . . ." His voice trailed off.

Holt allowed himself a small smile. He wondered what other youngsters besides himself had carried boxes of cookies from Miss Phoebe to Woodruff's bachelor apartment in these later years. And for once Kane didn't seem to have a handy

Bible quotation — one to cover throwing an old woman out of her home!

The judge turned his awful, glaring left eye on Reginald Bailey. "Miss Phoebe's lived with Adelaide as long as I can remember. Just where had you planned to send her?"

Reginald kept his eyes on the floor and his tongue between his teeth.

His mouth tight in an angry line, Woodruff pulled the docket sheet to him, whipped out his pen and began to scratch.

Judges, Holt reminded himself, didn't decide matters on the basis of emotional appeal. Except when some young whippersnapper tried to throw Miss Phoebe out of her home!

Finally the judge finished writing and looked over the bench. "I'm not granting anyone the right to vote decedent's stock," he announced. "You can put off your shareholders' meeting until after the probate hearing, which is set for Monday a week at nine a.m."

"Thank you, Judge," Holt said. The way things had gone there for a while, he regarded the postponement as a victory.

"I haven't finished," Woodruff said curtly. "Didn't you file an application to be appointed temporary administrator?"

Holt nodded uncertainly.

"Well, you can draw an order naming yourself. No power to vote the stock. Just the usual provisions for taking possession and preserving."

Holt's spirits leaped. He had his foot in the door if the temporary administration had to be extended.

The baleful glare of the judge's left eye aimed at Reg, seemed to galvanize that young man.

"In particular, Mr. Lawson," Judge Woodruff rasped, "you will take charge of decedent's home and see that no one disturbs its present occupant!"

Reg flinched.

Holt stuffed his papers in his briefcase. Dad had taught him not to stand around jawing and give a judge the chance to change his mind, once he ruled in your favor.

"Just a minute, Holt," the judge rapped out. "I want to see you in my chambers — to, ah, turn over that purse that's jammed into my safe."

In the judge's office, Woodruff got Adelaide's tremendous bag from his metal cabinet and passed it across the table. "Now maybe I'll have room for some of my own stuff," he observed.

Holt picked up the bag and was ready to go. But Judge Woodruff leaned back in his chair and propped his feet up on his desk. For once he seemed undisturbed at Holt's towering above him.

"Now that the fireworks are over," the judge said, "I want the straight story on that will."

"I haven't even had a chance to read it," Holt replied. "I took Adelaide's safe to Dallas and got it opened just in time to get back here."

"You're leveling?"

"Judge, I swear to you that will came out of Adelaide's safe. It's not something I cooked up."

Judge Woodruff drummed his fingers on the arms of his chair. There's something about that will," he said. "When you've been on the bench as long as I have, you sense things. The way Kane handled himself. The way he has Townsend lined up."

Holt felt an uneasy prickling sensation. He'd held out a bank loan, salary raise, even a consulting fee from the bakery to Townsend; and still the banker had taken sides with Reg. Impatient with chatter, he shifted restlessly from foot to foot.

Woodruff observed through his mild brown eye. "I don't suppose I'll be seeing much of you if you don't probate this will, Holt. Kane will take what's left of your law practice, and you'll pull out of Pinewood."

Putting it baldly stung to the quick. Holt had been smarting at the thought, knew it was true. "How about letting me worry about that?" he said shortly.

"Oh, I will, I will," the jurist assured him. "And you can let me worry whether Pinewood's got a new set of kingmakers and I've started off doing them wrong. They're entitled to sell Adelaide's Breads if that will's no good."

"I understand that."

"Then understand this, too." The diminutive judge got to his feet and brought his walleye to bear. "A week from Monday you come in and prove up that will or I'm going to turn the temporary administration over to Reginald Bailey — with full power to sell Adelaide's Breads!"

Chapter 13

Holt stepped out of the judge's chambers grimly clenching Adelaide's large bag in one hand and his briefcase in the other.

The ultimatum he'd just received made it certain that in ten days one of two things would happen: either he'd step into Adelaide's shoes or Reg would get the nod. And in that latter case, he could kiss good-bye to the retainers that were keeping his law office open and start packing.

In the courtroom Kane lingered about the counsel table. Holt felt his muscles brace, a tightening in his loins. One thing he knew — he'd bust a gut before he'd let that damned shyster grab off the remainder of his law practice and rout him out of town!

The big lawyer turned, flicked an inner switch, and his pale blue eyes lighted. "You don't mind if I sit in on the inventory, do you, Holt?"

Unusual civility for Kane, just after he'd lost a hearing! Holt observed his opponent narrowly. "That's your privilege," he conceded.

"I'll give you a hand." Kane stretched a long arm toward Adelaide's purse.

Instinctively Holt gripped the handle more tightly. "If this is what you're interested in, I'll inventory it here and now."

"You're in a hell of a hurry."

Holt nodded. "That's right."

He cursed the necessity mentally even as he agreed, however. The trail to Adelaide's witnesses began in Hilma. But before he could take off for there, he had to dictate an order, file the will, arrange a bond . . . hell, he had a dozen things to do.

Crossing to the counsel table, he opened the big bag and began lifting out it's contents.

Comb, brush, keys. Kane started sorting the items on the table.

Holt gave his adversary a sharp look. Just after Adelaide's death, Kane had been ready to attack him to get hold of the purse. Pulling the trifles back out of reach, he snapped, "Don't handle the merchandise!"

"Touchy, aren't you?" Kane scoffed.

Ignoring the remark, Holt continued to grope in the purse and bring forth items that he lined up on the table. A bundle of hairpins. Old-fashioned rouge box. The vial of nitroglycerin pills. More pills, lying loose. Half a dozen secretarial books such as Burgess used. The jewelry George White had stripped from Adelaide's body and packed away. Lint and spilled pills and more hairpins.

"There's nothing there worth inventorying except the jewelry," Kane said, turning away.

"Right. Two rings, the brooch, and a watch. I'll put it in the bank on my way to the office."

"As far as I'm concerned, you can give the purse to Miss Phoebe — throw it away — whatever you want." Kane walked off.

Holt nodded absently. Kane hadn't even asked to check the contents of Adelaide's safe! And the big lawyer was done with the purse itself when Holt wouldn't let him rake over its

140

contents.

It was out of character for Kane. Something about the whole situation rang very, very wrong.

What to do about it? Holt frowned, then grinned.

Because the starting place was obvious, when you stopped to think about it; and he knew now that he wasn't about to throw or give that big bag away until he'd gone through those notebooks with a fine toothed comb!

Still running in high gear, Holt reached home at eight. Burgess and he had finally licked the pile of work that seemed to stack up the moment he tried to leave town.

Tired and yet unable to relax, he began to mix himself a scotch and soda. Snubby, in turn, bounced around in front of the refrigerator indicating that dinner was overdue. Putting down a can of dog food, Holt finished making his drink and went into the front room.

Adelaide's big tapestry bag lay on the sofa beside his briefcase. Eyeing it, Holt debated whether he'd rather wade through Adelaide's memoranda at once or lug the stack of notebooks to Hilma. The scotch and soda disappeared.

Taking a long breath, Holt carried the bag to the kitchen table, turned it upside down and shook out the contents. The hotchpotch Adelaide had carried covered the table.

Laying aside the notebooks and loose memoranda, he put the other articles back in the purse. A litter of hairpins, the loose pellets, and scraps of dress materials remained. He brushed the clutter into a wastebasket.

The notebooks were crammed with figures on differential freight rates, sugar futures and other meaninglessness. But Holt poured over every page looking for the answers to two questions: First, where to find the witnesses to Adelaide's will? Second, what other reason, if any, made Kane so anxious to get his hands on that big tapestry bag?

141

Two hours of lost labor. Holt chucked the notebooks back into the purse, carried it to the front room and pushed the lamp on the small center table aside to make a place for it.

The clock on the mantle showed it to be almost ten. If he was going out of town, he ought to phone Connie. But just thinking about that afternoon — her father's giving him the lie — Connie's running out on him — set him to seething.

He started to the kitchen for a nightcap. At that moment the phone at the foot of the stairs rang.

It was Connie, sounding strained. "Holt, I can't go to sleep until I make you understand about this afternoon."

Despite all his efforts, he couldn't keep the rancor from his voice. "I understand, all right. Your father was out to worm himself in with Reg. He counted on you to handle me."

"It wasn't like that, Holt. Dad's desperate for money, and the sale was the only way to get it quickly."

"From Reg's stock?" Holt glanced at his briefcase where he had Fox's certificate stashed. "He doesn't have any."

"Reg told us about that. But he was to get everything above what he owed."

Holt's patience snapped. "Connie," he exploded, "I can't understand everybody's being so hell-bent on selling Adelaide's Breads. Talk about killing the goose that laid the golden egg . . ."

"I wish *you* were up here in this house!" Connie flared. Then her voice broke. "I just know Dad's going to have a breakdown. Holt, you should have let that sale go through!"

"I should, should I? And used what for us to get married on?"

There was silence at the other end of the line for a few moments. Then Connie sighed. "Holt, will it be all over in ten days?"

Holt grimaced. "It will so far as Judge Woodruff is concerned. Of course, you can appeal."

An almost frantic note came into Connie's voice. "Holt! You don't mean this could go on and on!"

He tried to put himself in her place — in that big house with her father driving her distracted. His irritation began to dissolve.

"Connie, Connie," he soothed. "Stick it out a few days and I'll be back. Things will work out."

"Well . . ." A quick, forced buoyancy. "Hurry, Holt . . . and remember, I love you."

"I love you, too," Holt said.

He felt sure that he meant it. Connie was all right. It was old man Townsend who was the fly in the ointment. Still, he found himself reviewing the many reasons why Connie was eminently desirable. That quality of loyalty she exhibited toward her father would be her husband's. Even if one didn't make a fetish of an hymeneal maidenhead, a man who'd had Trix could use a wife with Connie's decency. And certainly it would be a status symbol to have the Princess of Pinewood for a wife.

Holt shook his head. It was almost as though he seemed to need to reassure himself.

When Holt hit the sack, the nervous energy he'd been running on flicked off. He fell asleep almost at once.

Then a *yap, yap, yap* began to chase sleep away. Pulling a pillow over his ear, he fought for more rest. But Snubby wouldn't stop that infernal yipping.

Holt sat up in bed and shook his head. "What the hell . . .?"

Snubby dashed at the closed bedroom door and redoubled his clamor. Now Holt came wide awake. Snubby heard or smelled someone in the house!

143

Putting his feet over the side of the bed, he started up. Then he paused. He wasn't about to walk into another trap like Gino's!

But the revolver Gino had dropped might prove handy in the present situation . . .

Leaving the room in darkness, Holt crossed to the bureau. His fingers located the gun hiding amid his wool sports shirts.

He eased the bedroom door open. Snubby slid through and dashed down the stairs barking. Padding to the stairway, Holt peered below.

Utter darkness. Downstairs, the Peke's nails clicked across the kitchen linoleum. His bark turned to a fierce growl. Someone cursed. Then Holt heard a thud. Snubby yelped once, barked fiercely. There was the sound of a fresh attack.

Flicking on the light, Holt raised the revolver and charged to Snubby's aid. Halfway down the stairs a wire caught his ankles, cut his legs from under him. He pitched forward.

Even as he fell, however, he curled into a ball, pulling his arms and legs in and letting himself roll. But he hit the landing at the foot of the stairs, head first. Dazed, he tried to pull himself up.

Quick steps sounded in the back of the house. Holt got to his feet and wobbled to the kitchen. Empty. He made his way to the back door. No sign of the intruder.

Rallying, he shook his head, blinked his eyes, and began a closer inspection of things. Adelaide's notebooks lay neatly stacked on the kitchen table. Holt frowned. He remembered leaving them in her purse on the front room table.

Then he saw the big tapestry bag itself. Half hidden under the stove, open, it had spilled its other contents onto the kitchen floor. Holt knelt and began to pick up the now familiar odds and ends and spread them on the kitchen table. Bundle of hairpins. Rouge box. Loose memoranda.

"Damn!" Holt breathed. He didn't doubt that Kane had

finally succeeded in getting his hands on the purse. Snubby's attack must have interrupted a search begun on the kitchen table. The question was, had Kane got what he was after . . . something Holt had missed?

He sorted the items on the table. In his mind he went over the contents of Adelaide's purse, trying to figure what Kane had been so hot to get hold of.

But it was all there, except the jewelry, and Kane knew that was at the bank. And, except for the junk in the wastebasket. All there — notebooks, rouge, . . .

Suddenly Holt sucked in a sharp breath. Not all there! Adelaide's vial of nitroglycerin pills was missing!

But why? Kane wouldn't have wanted a vial of nitroglycerin pills. He had his own.

Pondering, Holt walked slowly to the front room. Up the stairs, where he'd tripped, a wire stretched across the stairway from one of the banisters to a nail stuck between the wall and the base mold. Someone . . ., he'd bet it was Kane . . . had rigged a neat booby trap! Kane must have wanted something desperately to have taken the risk.

Returning to the kitchen, Holt stooped and scanned every inch of the floor. No vial. That had to be what Kane had taken. And if not for nitroglycerin pills, . . . for what else?

Holt whirled. The kitchen wastebasket with the clutter of loose pills, hairpins and scraps of cloth stood in a corner. He carefully poured the litter onto the kitchen table and eyed it thoughtfully.

If Kane hadn't been after Adelaide's nitroglycerin pills, then how about the pills Burgess had spilled from Kane's hand into Adelaide's purse? And, when Kane found no loose tablets in the purse, what more natural than for him to assume someone had put them in the vial?

The tiny white disks lying on the kitchen table looked

like Adelaide's nitroglycerin pills. Holt felt a quiver of revulsion. They also looked exactly like the strychnine tablets most Pinewood boys had seen farmers use to make rat poison!

A thought occurred that was so despicable Holt started to dismiss it from his mind. He turned away from the table. Kane wouldn't have poisoned Adelaide!

Now sleep was out of the question. Holt called the airport in Tyler. A flight that would start him toward Hilma left in less than two hours.

As he shaved, he argued with himself. Why would Kane just happen to be carrying rat poison pills? People in Pinewood didn't murder or poison each other. And, even if Kane were capable of it, wouldn't he wait until after the trial? Was his ego so great he couldn't stand losing a lawsuit to Holt?

Finally, dressed and packed, Holt dialed Burgess's number.

The burr-r-ring sound repeated a half dozen times before Burgess came on the line with a sleepy, "Hello".

"This is Holt. Can I come by for a minute?"

Shock-sputters from Burgess. "Holt! What time is it? Have you been drinking?"

"Nothing so pleasant." He glanced at his wristwatch. "It's five-thirty, and I'm leaving for the airport."

"Give me a couple of minutes."

Holt put his suitcase on the back porch. His briefcase lay on the sofa. Hefting it thoughtfully, he stowed Gino's revolver in one of the side pockets and put case with grip.

Then he got a clean envelope out of the drawer of the living room table and went into the kitchen.

After a final moment of debate, he swept the loose pills into the envelope and sealed the flap.

The front door of Burgess's house was open. Holt

understood he was not to rouse the household by ringing and stepped inside.

In a moment Burgess came in wearing a blue dressing gown and a sleepy, soft, luscious look.

"I didn't think you were leaving for hours," she said. "Can I fix you some coffee?"

Calling his thoughts to heel before they started romping off, Holt shook his head. "Somebody broke into the house, rifled that purse of Adelaide's and took her vial of pills."

"Have you called the police?"

"And spend a couple of hours answering questions?" Holt reached in his pocket and handed over his envelope. "I want you to keep this. It's tablets I found in the bottom of Adelaide's bag."

Burgess raised her eyebrows. "What do I do with them?"

"Haven't you read any modern detective stories? You run one through an electronic lab and find out the killer was a left-handed ballplayer from Kalamazoo."

"Seriously, Holt!"

He looked her in the face. "Kane looted that purse, Burgess. He offered to fight for it in Woodruff's office. This afternoon he made a big fuss about 'inventorying' it, but he completely forgot to worry about the contents of Adelaide's safe, where the real valuables would be."

Burgess gestured with the envelope. "This is supposed to tell us why?"

"Maybe. Have you thought how coincidental it was that Adelaide had her fatal heart attack at *just* the moment she was putting the kibosh on Reg's suit? Not the next day. Not even half an hour later."

"Well, — but Kane *was* pounding at her."

"You bet he was. And nobody could stop him until he'd upset her so that it brought one of her spells on. That's how he managed to slip her a pill."

Burgess furrowed her brow and took her lower lip between her teeth. Then she spoke uncertainly, "Holt, I think I was the one who put the pill in her mouth."

Studying her reaction, Holt noted with satisfaction that she didn't summarily reject the theory he was building. "I know," he said. "I've gone over it in my mind a dozen times. But it was Kane who produced the pills. You grabbed for them, spilled some in Adelaide's purse, and put one under her tongue."

Burgess continued to ponder for a few moments. Then she smiled and shook her head. "Holt, this is Pinewood. Kane teaches a Sunday School class — he's been promiment for years. Now doesn't your notion sound far-fetched?"

Holt twisted the corner of his mouth up in a wry smile.

"It does at that," he admitted. "Which is why you're going to tell Doc the chemical analysis has to be top secret — when you take the pellets out of that envelope by his clinic."

Chapter 14

On Friday afternoon Holt arrived at Hilma's one-strip airport in a small, single-engine plane.

The young man at the controls taxied the plane up to the field's single building. "Remember now, I ran you over as a favor. They're rough about hiring out 'fore you pass your commercial."

Holt got out his wallet and handed over a ten dollar bill. "Don't worry. I really appreciate your bringing me down."

Brad Oates came forward as soon as the propeller stopped whirling. "Gosh, Holt, it's good to see you."

None of the banter with which Brad had always filled the locker room. No thumping on the back. In spite of the crisp dry warmth, Holt felt a chill. "You still haven't turned them up?"

Brad shook his head. He led the way to a Falcon sedan and crammed himself into the front seat.

Keenly disappointed, Holt followed and squeezed in beside him. But what the hell — did he expect Brad to latch onto Davenport or Jenkins in twenty-four hours?

Brad started the car toward town. "You understand, I haven't had a chance to check the desk registers myself. And someone *could* have moved to town and out again in a month or two without my getting acquainted."

Holt seized on the hopes held out. "Here's what we'll do. First, hire some help. You head a team looking for possible short time residents. Check the post office, telephone company, churches, . . ."

Brad held up a huge hand. "I've got the signal, captain. A study in depth."

Holt gave the big shoulder that hunched over the wheel a punch. "My team will look for transients. We'll make a personal check of the register of every hotel, motel, dude ranch, or what-have-you out here."

"You make me feel young again. 'Come on, Brad. Get your ass into it. We only need one more yard.' That's Lawson."

"We'll do okay, Brad." Now Holt was smiling, full of go. "We don't even have to actually locate Davenport or Jenkins. I can squeeze past probate requirement if we turn up a couple of characters that knew them and are willing to identify their signatures."

"Okay, captain." Brad sounded more cheerful. He stepped on the accelerator, and the car picked up speed.

For the next five days Holt worked almost around the clock. Wednesday evening after dinner Brad and he went back to Brad's office and compared notes. The day had been spent recrossing their tracks.

"You might as well face it," Brad said. "We're spinning our wheels."

Holt let his head droop in a gesture of assent. Glumly certain that he was overdrawing his account, he wrote out checks for the helpers and accepted Brad's offer of a lift.

The hotel's wide veranda was deserted when Brad pulled his car in alongside.

"Come in for a drink?" Holt asked. Low in spirits, he couldn't put much enthusiasm into the invitation.

150

Brad shook his head. "No thanks. It'll be better if I go off and bleed by myself."

Holt stopped by the cubby hole that doubled as baggage room and service desk. The young pimp who also hawked newspapers in the square was sprawled over the counter, the soiled sack that hung across his narrow shoulders now empty.

Pushing in beside him, Holt tried to catch Manuel's eye. The bellboy stood behind the counter, his round, unwrinkled face now furrowed in concentration. Three shells stood on a napkin spread across the counter.

In spite of his gloom, Holt smiled, remembering how Manuel had played games with Reg and himself on their visits with Adelaide in years past. Now Manuel, with his unaging swarthy complexion and jet-black hair, seemed unchanged — except for a bulge at the waistline of his uniform that his love for tequila might have brought.

Manuel looked up.

"Get me plane reservations in the morning to Tyler, Manuel," Holt instructed. "And bring me some ice and soda in my room."

"Right away," Manuel promised. Then his gaze returned to the three shells, and he laid a half dollar on the counter.

Waiting for his ice and soda, Holt paced the floor and tried not to look ahead to Monday's hearing.

But Kane strutted the courtroom. Reg simpered. Townsend fawned. And Connie . . .

The picture lacerated Holt's mind. He poured a slug of Scotch into a thimble-sized glass, drank it with tap water, and made a face. Old times notwithstanding, he was going to call the desk clerk and raise hell if Manuel didn't tear himself away from that shell game and get his ass up here.

A knock at the door. Manuel brought in a tray with a bucket of ice, two quarts of sparkling water and glass of

151

serviceable height.

For some reason not entirely clear to himself, Holt over tipped with a dollar bill, then mixed himself a decent drink and settled in the easy chair to enjoy it.

The phone on the bed table jangled. Holt pulled himself up.

The desk clerk sounded hesitant. "Operator says she's ready on a call to Pinewood, Mr. Lawson. I don't have a record of one. I thought maybe you . . ."

Holt heard Manuel's voice, faint but distinct, sputtering at the clerk. "That's not Senor Lawson's call. I can tell you about it . . ."

"Never mind, Mr. Lawson," the desk clerk said. "It was a mistake."

You're damn right it was, Holt thought. He slapped his drink on the dresser and strode down the hall to the elevator.

The street Arab was still hanging around Manuel's counter. As he approached, Holt saw Manuel seize a shell, turn it up and expose bare napkin. A grimy hand snatched up a dollar bill and stuffed it in the young gyp's pocket.

Manuel pulled his wallet out and extracted a five dollar bill. Sweat glistened on his swarthy forehead.

The scene suggested a course of action that might be productive. Changing direction, Holt continued down the corridor to the liquor store. He could always come back to the idea of slapping Manuel around.

The salesman in the liquor store was thoroughly familiar with Manuel's preferences. Provided with a pint of tequila and a sack of lemons, Holt returned to the service desk.

A dollar lay on the napkin. The sharper covered the pea and weaved his shells. Even knowing the trick, Holt sensed rather than saw the shell tip slightly and the pea escape into the spot between thumb and second finger, concealed by the forefinger.

152

Manuel had his eyes fixed on the peas. The con artist paused. Unerringly seizing the shell that had covered the pea, Manuel flipped it over and exposed its emptiness.

"That was it," he protested.

The grimy hand grabbed up one of the other shells, at the same time dropping the pea so it appeared to have lain there.

Manuel's shoulders sagged; but his eyes glittered with a fever, and he reached for his wallet.

"You're being a sucker, Manuel," Holt observed.

The street Arab turned. Yellow teeth showed in an obsequious smile. "Mister, we're just playing a game."

Manuel shoved his wallet back in his pocket. "Is it a trick, Senor Holt?"

"It's a straight out gyp."

The skinny young man let out a sort of hiss. His filthy hand came out with a long handled knife.

But Holt clamped down on the hand before the knife could open. Simultaneously, twisting the youth's arm, he turned the pocket with the money toward Manuel. "Take your dough," he said. "You got cheated."

Manuel licked his lips, then shook his head. "You better let him go. He's a tough kid."

With a sudden shove, Holt sent the boy sprawling. Then he turned and deliberately pocketed the three shells and peas. "These cost a buck," he said. "I guess Manuel's bought them several times over."

"I'm gonna get you," the kid promised.

The physical violence had done a world of good for Holt's spirits. He almost hoped for more of the same. Kicking the switchblade knife across the tile to the crouching young tough, he challenged, "So get me!"

The boy snatched up the knife, flicked it open and glared. The blood raced wildly in Holt's veins, and he grinned.

153

For a moment the boy crouched, glaring. Then he turned on his heel. "The hell with you," he snarled.

Holt drew in a deep breath and turned to Manuel. "Want to know the secret of the three shell game? Amaze your friends. Make them gasp. And pick up a few bucks on the side."

Manuel's eyes had a wide, fixed look. "You can show me how to work it?" He was completely hooked.

Holt smiled. "It's past your closing time. Come on up and I'll teach you the trick."

Back in his room, Holt made preparations for Manuel's arrival. He spread a sheet over the table so he'd have a surface that wasn't slick. Then he pulled up chairs for his spectator and himself and put tequila, lemons and ice close at hand.

A couple of hesitant raps sounded at the door. Manuel must have begun to worry about that Pinewood call.

"Come in!" Holt flung the door open and beamed his good will.

Manuel sidled in. Holt gestured toward the tray of tequila and lemons.

"Make yourself a drink," Holt invited.

"Well . . . maybe a small one." Manuel filled a glass with ice, squeezed in the juice of a lemon, poured a modest quantity of straight tequila, then added a dash more.

Watching, Holt winced and hastily drank some of his Scotch and soda.

Manuel sat down and for a few moments sipped steadily at his drink. Then he looked up at Holt. "You're going to show me how that shell game works?"

"Sure," Holt said. "Here, let me freshen your drink."

He took Manuel's glass, replenished the ice and lemon juice, then poured in tequila almost to the brim. Manuel took the glass without protest and began to work on it.

Holt sat down at the table and made his voice casual.

154

"Manuel, are you *sure* you never heard of Tom Davenport or Bruce Jennings?"

"I told you! I swear it!" Manuel put his glass on the table and pushed his chair back. "You just got me up here to ask me more questions!"

"Relax," Holt said. He took the pea and three shells out of his pocket and put them on the sheet. "This isn't going to be as professional as your pal's, but it'll give you the idea."

Manuel hunched his chair back to the table. Holt covered the pea with a shell, went through the serpentine motions and slipped the pea into hiding the way Theodore Calhoun had demonstrated in the magic shop.

Manuel grabbed the shell and found it empty. "You can do it!" he exclaimed. "Show me. Show me."

"I am," Holt assured him. "Let's finish our drinks."

Now Manuel relaxed and drank freely. He seemed reassured about Holt.

After a while Holt noted that Manuel was sitting in a carefully balanced position. He wondered if the tequila was taking effect. "By the way, did you get my reservations?" he asked.

Manuel raised his eyebrows and pulled his head back as though trying to bring his eyes into focus. "Si, senor. It is all in your box."

He formed his words with careful exactness. Holt permitted himself the pleasure of a small, brief, secret smile, then moved on to a new approach: "Manuel, the summer we've talked about — sometime Miss Bailey got together with two men and signed a will. They had to be men just passing through town. And she wouldn't have bumped into them anywhere except at the hotel."

"O-o-oh! *That* evening!" Manuel seemed happy that Holt had phrased a question he could answer. "On that evening Miss Bailey sent Senor Reginald to find two men to witness

155

her will and he came down to the lobby and he walked up to two men and he asked them if they would witness a will and then they all went up to Miss Bailey's room. I do not know anything else."

Straining forward in his chair, Holt stored away in his mind every detail of the pat story Manuel had obviously committed to memory and now gave word for word. Here at last was something more than a void, and Holt felt his heart beat quicken in response.

With slow, deliberate motions, Manuel reached for his glass, brought it carefully to his lips, drank, and returned the tumbler to its exact position.

"What time of day did this happen?" Holt asked.

Manuel drew himself erect and puffed his cheeks. "I do not know anything else," he repeated like a parrot.

Holt shrugged his shoulders, brushed the pea and shells into his hand and pocketed the trick.

"You promised to show me!" Manuel protested.

"To keep you from being hoaxed." Holt gave a short laugh. "And here you are trying to hoax me."

"No!" Manuel's eyes came into better focus. "I swear it. I have not lied to you!"

"No? Why did you call Pinewood tonight?"

"I did not . . ." Manuel shrugged. "Senor Reg gave me twenty dollars to tell him when you were leaving. And . . ."

"And to find out if you'd had a chance to give me that song-and-dance about his picking up a couple of witnesses in the lobby." Holt scoffed. "You know from A to Z how Reg picked up these men in the lobby and can't remember what time of day it was!"

"It was . . ." Manuel wet his lips. "It was about eight at night."

"Did the men eat dinner here?"

"No." Now Manuel spoke very precisely as though the

alcohol had aroused a need for exactness. "They had just come in."

"So Reg walks past a half dozen permanent guests that would be sitting around that time of day, by-passes you and the desk clerk, and tackles a couple of complete strangers?"

As he spoke, Holt took the three shell game from his pocket and spread it out on the table in front of Manuel.

"Well . . ." Manuel hesitated, eyed the pea and shells. "Senor Reg seemed to know a man they were with."

Holt tensed. "What did the men look like, Manuel?"

Manuel shook his head and reared back in his chair. "I do not know anything else!"

Brushing two of the shells aside, Holt covered the pea with the third shell and pushed it right under Manuel's nose. As he did, he let the back of the shell tip up and caught the pea between his thumb and second finger so that his forefinger concealed it from Manuel.

For a moment Manuel stared at the solitary shell. Then he grabbed it up and stared at the bare cloth. Running a finger inside the shell, he felt its thickness.

Then he turned to Holt. "You will show me? You swear it?"

Holt nodded.

"The two men . . ." Manuel shrugged. "They looked like anybody else. The third man . . . he caught the eye."

Holt hunched forward, sitting on the edge of his chair. "What was so special about him, Manuel?"

"He was tall — taller than you. He almost filled the elevator by himself. And his eyes — like a fire burning in ice."

An arm on the table, Holt leaned across toward Manuel. "That third man — he had bushy eyebrows and a shock of gray hair?"

"That is the one!" Manuel exclaimed.

Holt slammed his fist on the table. "Kane!" he exploded. "That bastard Kane! He's had this trap set up all the time!"

157

Chapter 15

Manuel's information kept Holt twisting unhappily from side to side long after he'd stretched out on the bed to try to sleep.

Now he knew the flaw in Adelaide's will! Kane had slipped a couple of frauds into town, put them through the farce of acting as witnesses, and whisked them away. Witnesses meant not to be found. A will foredoomed not to be probated.

Writhing, Holt shifted from one hard, sweaty spot to another; just as his mind raced back and forth, back and forth, seeking a way out of the trap.

Early Thursday morning he phoned Brad Oates at home.

Brad didn't sound at all sleepy. "I've been up an hour," he explained. "I'm going to San Antonio today."

Holt frowned. "I may need your help this week-end."

"I'll be back tomorrow. You turn something up?"

Holt summarized his session of the night before with Manuel.

"They gave him twenty bucks to feed me the story they'd cooked up to cover Reg if I came across their tracks," he concluded. "I don't think Manuel had any other connection."

"You're probably right. What can I do?"

"If I try for a postponement Monday, I want Manuel there to tell his story. If I send you a distress signal, get him there whether it takes flattery, bribery or a knock on the head."

"I can handle Manuel." Brad sounded confident. "I know his whole family."

"Good. Maybe you better take a sworn statement from him — just in case."

"I'll handle it. Have you come up with any ideas for finding those witnesses?"

Holt gripped the receiver until his fingers ached. A sudden warmth covered his body just under the skin.

"I'll tell you how I'll find them," he blazed. "I'll choke it out of that damned, sniveling Reg!"

Brad cleared his throat. Then, "I'm not trying to call the signals, Holt. But juries don't like the guy that uses a rubber hose. If I were trying the case against you, I'd make sure the jury knew how you collected your evidence."

Holt exploded. "Dammit, can't you see what they've done? I can't puncture this story they've trumped up if I just put Reg on the stand and ask him pretty please?"

Brad's silence indicated he hadn't changed his mind. And if Brad's reaction was negative, what would Woodruff's be? The judge had given full warning of what he'd do if Holt, an officer of his court, got out of line again.

"Think about it," Brad urged. "You got Manuel to talk without roughing him up."

Holt scowled. Leaning on Manuel in a hotel room was one thing; cross-examining Reg in open court under Kane's watchful eye, another. And no one knew that better than he.

No. What he needed was muscle, pure and simple; muscle, plus a way to apply it that wouldn't bring repercussions from Judge Woodruff.

Only that constituted an impossible contradiction, on the

160

face of it, unless —

Inspiration, alive and breathing.

Because, now that he stopped to think of it, he *had* muscle: belligerent, professional quality talent just begging to be used.

Abruptly, Holt stopped scowling; started grinning.

He said, "There's a character in Dallas who is very persuasive with Reg. He's got forty thousand bucks riding on this case. And I guarantee you neither the judge nor the jury could hold me responsible for what he does."

"You're on the beam," Brad said. "Good luck, captain."

Holt hung up.

Now his only problem was to convince Fox that the gambler would have to cooperate if he wanted to see his money.

Five hours later Holt alighted at Dallas' Love Field airport and took a taxi direct to the bus depot. Tiers of coin-operated lockers lined the walls. Holt dropped a quarter in one and stored his grip.

Thoughtfully he hefted his briefcase. Gino's revolver weighed heavily. After a moment's consideration, Holt left the gun in the locker with the grip. Gino's rod couldn't insure cooperation out of Fox and might get matters off to a bad start.

All the phone booths were occupied with gabbers who appeared to be killing time until bus departures. Waiting, Holt began to check the phone book for Fox's address. The gambler was openly listed in the alphabetical directory as "Arthur Fox atty" although he had shunned further publicity in the yellow pages' classification, "Attorneys".

Finally one of the windbags ran out of air. Holt got a collect call to Burgess placed.

Operator identified the person wanting to charge the call,

and Burgess came on the line with an eager, "Hello. Why haven't you called? How'd you make out?"

"Look, Burgess, neither town's had dial phones long enough for me to lose that feeling of togetherness with Operator."

There was a pause at Burgess's end of the line. Then, in a cool, controlled tone, she said, "I've got some lab reports for you here."

Holt started. Doc's analysis on the pills in Adelaide's purse! But he put down his intense interest. Reg dated one of the telephone operators, and a full report might mean something to him.

"That can keep. How about meeting the early evening bus? I left my car at the airport in Tyler."

"Okay." Burgess's business-like manner dismissed the lab reports as routine matter.

"One other thing. I'm about to call on an attorney here. Gentleman named Fox."

"I know who you mean," Burgess assured him.

Holt gave her the number of Fox's office. "If I don't call you back in thirty minutes, I'd suggest you get in touch with me there. I'm not sure how the conference will go."

"Will do. See you tonight." Burgess rang off.

The lobby directory carried Fox's office number, sandwiched in among the loan sharks, divorce detectives, and ambulance chasers who'd taken over the ornate building as prestige tenants abandoned it for more modern quarters.

Fox's entrance, a gleaming eyesore of glass and black marble, stood out against the drab surroundings like a new car in an auto salvage yard. Holt waded through lush white carpet to the desk of a blonde receptionist.

"Holt Lawson to see Mr. Fox," he told her.

Ice-cold blue eyes appraised him. For a moment Holt

162

wasn't sure his message had gotten through. There was an unpierceableness about the girl. Silver hair, drawn back severely into a bun, framed her face like a helmet and pulled pretty features into hard, expressionless lines.

The effect was such as to give Holt an urge to yank out the bobby pins and tousle her hair so it fell down around her shoulders.

"Mr. Fox is busy." The pale, frozen face didn't change expression, and the snug-fitting metallic dress glinted like armor as the girl turned away. "You want to leave a message?"

"Sure, I'll leave a message." Holt shoved her silver ash tray aside, plopped his briefcase down and squatted on the edge of the desk. "You tell Fox I came in to help him collect forty thousand bucks, but I didn't like the treatment I got from the snotty dame parked out front."

The blonde blinked. Holt made as if to get up.

"Just a minute!" she blurted.

Holt grinned. It hadn't been hard to find a soft spot. And he stood willing to bet you could find even softer ones if you took a can opener to that dress.

The blonde picked up a phone with a box-like contraption into which she began talking. Holt tried to hear what she was saying, but the box affair muffled her voice. He shifted his weight restlessly.

Listening, the girl looked Holt over and nodded.

"Tell Fox to save the 'in-conference-sit-down-and-wait' routine," Holt warned. "I haven't got the time."

Hastily the girl addressed herself to the box again. Then, hanging up, she gestured toward a door. "Mr. Fox will see you in the library."

Holt collected his briefcase and went into the room she'd indicated.

The room stank of stale drinks and cigarette stubs left to

burn themselves out. A low, shaded bulb lighted a round table that was covered with green felt cloth. Poker chips and cards lay scattered among the overflowing ash trays.

Holt grimaced at the look and smell of the "library". Several framed certificates hung on the side wall. He went over and inspected them. Fox had collected a bachelor of laws degree, New York and Texas law licenses, and some sort of testimonial from a New York welfare agency.

Looking back at the rank remains of last night's gambling, Holt felt a revulsion for Fox's swanky lay-out. He believed in feathering one's nest, but a man could give up too much.

At the far end of the room, some shelves built around a door housed a scattering of books. Holt started over to see what Fox had selected for his pocket law library.

Just then the door opened. Gino walked in.

Hesitating, Holt studied the heavy, handsome face for some hint of what reception was intended. Gino's sensual lips parted in a smile, and he waved a massive arm toward a chair.

"Sit down," the young hood said. "Mr. Fox will be right in."

Holt started back to the table.

Then Gino looked toward the door from the reception room. "Mr. Fox," he said, "did you sign those contracts?"

Holt turned to face Fox. No one was there. Not a muscle's movement telegraphed the punch Gino threw. But Holt caught a left in the belly that doubled him over.

Then Gino swung a club-like fist from below the waist. The blow rammed Holt's chin. His head snapped back. Dazed and winded, he dropped to one knee.

Gino grabbed a wrist, wrenched it backward, and pulled out a set of handcuffs.

"What the hell . . ." Holt panted. But before he could get himself organized his hands were cuffed behind and he was sitting precariously on the edge of a chair, facing his broad-shouldered assailant.

Smiling mockingly, Gino pulled the green felt cloth from under the ash tray and glasses. He knotted the stinking, suffocating cloth around Holt's head.

A door clicked open and closed again. Holt recognized Fox's voice.

"Oh, come now," Fox said indulgently, "take that thing off so I can talk to him. I'm sure Mr. Lawson gets the idea."

The cloth was whipped away. Holt blinked, gasped, tried to shake the fuzziness out of his head.

Looking amused, Fox circled the table and sat on its edge. "You know, Gino did have you fixed up exactly like he was at your house."

Holt lurched awkwardly to his feet. His stomach churned angrily. The furious pounding of blood in his temples drove out rational thought.

Across the room, Gino shrugged his coat so it hung perfectly and looked pleased with himself.

Holt measured the distance to Gino. He wanted nothing in life but to accomplish a flying butt that would ram the dark young hood's belly into his backbone.

Fox shrugged, stood and started out. "There's no use trying to talk to you now."

"Hold it!" Breathing deeply, Holt got a grip on his temper. The hell with letting a brawl cost him Monday's battle in the courtroom.

Fox turned back, sat on the edge of the table, and lifted an eyebrow inquiringly.

Settling on a chair, Holt tried to look as business-like as he could with his hands cuffed behind him. "Our deal is, if I probate the Bailey will Monday, I buy the stock you got from Reg for forty thousand bucks."

Fox nodded, said nothing, and watched Holt attentively.

"You'll have to get me the names of the witnesses for me to probate it," Holt said. "Reg ran in a couple of guys with phony names."

Fox drummed his fingers on the table for a few moments, then seemed to reach a decision. "I've got a better idea. Kane said the judge will okay the sale of the bakery if you *don't* probate the will Monday. I get my dough with no sweat."

Holt shook his head. "It won't work that way. I can prove Reg brought in the witnesses. Woodruff won't stand still for that sort of sharp practice. He'll give me more time, and you can whistle for your money."

Fox picked up a deck of cards and dealt himself a hand. His face had the careful look of a skillful player debating what cards to hold. Holt waited confidently. Fox wouldn't want delay.

Then Fox threw down the cards with an air of decision. Holt fixed his eyes on the gambler's face.

"Gino," Fox said, "Make our guest comfortable. He'll be with us a few days. And while you're baby sitting, I want to see you do some work on that extension course."

Holt started up. Gino moved between Fox and him.

"You're nuts, Fox," Holt declared. "You can't hold me."

"I'm already doing it," Fox pointed out. "And when you don't show for the Monday hearing, the judge will okay the sale of the bakeries and I'll get my dough."

Holt pulled his handcuffed arms to his side and twisted his head down to look at his wrist watch. Over thirty minutes had passed since he'd talked to Burgess. Why the hell didn't she call?

"By the way, Mr. Lawson," Fox said, "this new approach means I may need my stock certificate back. Where is it?"

Holt glanced toward his briefcase. Instantly he cursed himself for the stupid give-away — and for having brought the certificate with him in the first place.

Smiling, Fox unzipped the case, extracted the stock certificate and stuck it in his inner coat pocket.

"You're not playing it smart, Fox," Holt warned. "You know kidnapping's not worth the risk. And I've told my office where I am."

Fox snorted. "So you came in with a crazy proposition, and I turned you down. You know you're licked and you go on a binge. Soon as I get my money, a desk clerk will call your office to come get you out of his motel before he calls the cops."

Fox walked out. Holt frowned. The gambler's plan sounded workable. Who'd buy a kidnapping story from a man found dead drunk in some dump?

Calculating, Holt again measured the distance between him and Gino.

The dark young muscle man caught the look. Circling the chair, he hauled Holt to his feet and slammed him down again with the handcuffs behind the chair's back.

Frustrated, Holt jeered, "You do real good when I've got my hands tied behind me."

"Too bad we can't put any marks on you." Gino shoved the chair in under the table top.

Feeling his chest jammed against the table's edge, Holt realized the hopelessness of trying to jump his guard.

Gino went to the book shelves and brought a folder, notebook and text back to the table. Holt strained and twisted until he got his wristwatch out where he could see it.

"You have an appointment?" Gino asked with polite sarcasm.

Ignoring the crack, Holt tried to imagine how the conversation had gone when Burgess had called and gotten the brush-off from the frosty blonde outside.

Gino returned to his books, and the cupid's bow of his full lip pushed up and out as he wrestled with a section in his text.

Apparently Gino was settling for a long wait. Fox must be sitting tight until night when the building would empty. Thinking ahead, Holt realized that once they got him clear of the office, there'd be no way for anyone to find him. Perspiration began to flow freely down his body.

Gino looked up from his text book. "Do you know offhand if Texas is one of the states that has adopted the doctrine of imputed negligence?"

Holt gasped. Before he could choose between the amusement, annoyance and amazement that struck him, Fox dashed in.

The gambler ran slender fingers that trembled through his slick hair. Rounding the table, he leaned on it facing Holt.

"You want me to squeeze the names of those witnesses out of Bailey, right? He twisted his neck in nervous jerks.

Holt nodded. "Right!"

"You've got yourself a deal." The gambler turned to Gino. "Get those cuffs off. Quick."

For a moment Gino continued to sit, his mouth open.

Fox snapped his fingers impatiently. "C'mon, c'mon. We haven't got all day." He wheeled back to Holt. "Now you better hustle out front and tell those flatfeet that it's all a mistake, that your secretary's the hysterical type."

Gino fumbled the handcuffs loose. Holt stood and rubbed his wrists. Then he grinned sourly at Fox.

"I hate like hell to take you off the hook," Holt declared. "But I guess I'll have to, because if I leave you here answering questions for the cops, you can't be in Pinewood getting some answers for me."

He walked over to Fox, flipped open the coat of the gambler and extracted the stock certificate. Then, whistling happily, he went to square matters with Burgess's emissaries, the police.

Chapter 16

Holt walked from Fox's office to the bus station with a spring in his step. The calculating part of his mind warned him he was still a long way from getting out of Kane's trap. But he still felt an amazing buoyancy at having managed to stay in the game at all.

The bus hummed its way into East Texas at a steady seventy miles per hour. Forced to sit doing nothing, Holt's mood changed from one of buoyancy to grim determination. Once he had the names of the men Kane had palmed off on Adelaide — what then?

Gripping hard on the arm rest, he laid his plans. Such men would have a price, a fear of prison. Bribery or blackmail would get at least one of them to Monday's hearing!

It was growing dark when, a long two hours later, the bus lurched off the main highway and bounced over the dip onto the street leading to Pinewood's square. Holt snatched up his briefcase and valise. In a minute he'd have Doc's report on the pills taken from Adelaide's purse!

At Lone Star Drug and Bus Depot, Burgess had her aging coupe parked next to the bus stop. Holt swung down and strode toward it.

A mixed clamor of yelps and barks started up. Snubby

169

clawed at the car window.

Holt threw his things behind the car seat. To shut Snubby up, he let the Pekingese stand in his lap and lick his face. Burgess got the car under way without ado.

The moment they pulled away from the stop, Holt turned and demanded, "What did Doc say about those pills?"

"You were wrong, Holt. They weren't anything."

"What do you mean, 'they weren't anything'? They had to be something."

"They were saccharin . . . artificial sweetener. Couldn't hurt anybody."

Holt shook his head. "They weren't Adelaide's. She hated the stuff. Couldn't stand the aftertaste."

Something was wrong. Holt kept Snubby quiet with absent-minded petting. He'd started thinking of questions that had to have an answer.

What were strange saccharin pills doing in Adelaide's purse?

When Adelaide had recovered from a dozen angina spells, how plausible was the coincidence of the last one's leading to a fatal heart attack just as she was scuttling Reg's suit?

Why had the pill Burgess gave Adelaide produced, not relief, but that look of sudden terror?

Holt turned to Burgess.

"Burgess," he asked, "Do you know what brings on a heart attack?"

Burgess hesitated. "Why . . . stress, I've always heard."

"Right." Holt nodded. "Stress. Physical or emotional. So what happens if you're having angina pains and you don't get your nitroglycerin?"

"Well . . . the blood vessels would stay clogged . . . Do you mean that that and the continuing pain would have caused Adelaide's heart attack?"

"I mean that and more," Holt affirmed. "I mean that the

most upsetting, horrible, terror-fraught experience an old woman could have . . . an experience that would bring on a heart attack if anxiety ever has . . . would be to be in that fix and suddenly realize you'd been given a useless sugar pill . . . that someone was murdering you!"

Burgess put her hand on his forearm with a touch of gentle restraint. "Holt," she began, "you can't prove . . ."

He pulled his arm away. "I'm not losing my cool," he protested. "But I'm not going to call it the perfect crime and forget it. Kane murdered Adelaide just as surely as if those pills had been strychnine!"

Ahead, Holt's house came into view. But something about it wasn't right. Leaning forward, eyes narrowed, Holt studied it. It came to him, after a moment: The kitchen window was dark. But he always left the light over the sink on for Snubby and for his own return.

And from somewhere further inside the house came an unaccustomed glow.

Holt pivoted to Burgess. "Did you tell Connie I was coming in?"

Burgess turned her large brown eyes on him, briefly and stonily. "I did not. I just handle office appointments."

Could Fox have changed his mind and sent Gino to take him out of play? Or was Kane back for his missing pills?

"Keep going past the house," Holt instructed. "Turn the corner and let me out at the alley."

"What's the matter?"

"Somebody's in there. Or has been. I'm going to find out."

"Don't be silly, Holt. We'll get the police." Burgess made a right turn at the corner and stepped on the gas.

"And let them get away? The hell with that!" Holt reached over and switched off the ignition.

The car began to cough to a stop.

171

"No!" Burgess reached for the ignition key.

Holt pulled the key from its slot. Leaning over the back of the car seat, he got Gino's pistol out of the suitcase.

Burgess gasped. "Holt, listen. You're no gunman. Please . . ."

Holt slid out of the car. Burgess had tossed her tumbler of cold logic on an erupting volcano. For five days his body had screamed for physical action while he played guessing games about the who and where of witnesses.

Now, at last, he had a chance really to do something, perhaps catch Kane red-handed. He wasn't about to miss it.

Burgess had her hand stretched out. He pressed the car key into it.

"Now you get out of here," he ordered. Then, pivoting, he sprinted down the alley. Snubby came panting behind.

The alley gate stood closed. Holt vaulted it . . . dashed for the back porch steps.

The kitchen door was shut. Tearing up the stairs, Holt fumbled out his key, got the door open, flipped on the light.

Cabinets and drawers stood open. Careless of exposing himself, Holt ran on into the front part of the house.

Living room and dining room were empty. Holt paused uncertainly.

Now Snubby scurried in, stood a moment wheezing through his cocked-up nose, then raced up the stairs that led to the second floor.

Holt's uncertainty dissolved. Revolver cocked, he followed Snubby.

The Peke reached the top landing. There, with infuriating nonchalance, he sat down and looked up at his master as though to see what came next in the game.

Swearing under his breath, Holt checked the upstairs rooms . . . and found them empty. Upturned mattresses and ransacked drawers gave no clue as to how long the intruder

172

had been gone.

Finally, giving up, Holt descended the stairs. Back in the kitchen, in the same moment, a door latch clicked.

Holt went rigid. Then, bringing up his gun, he charged.

Burgess shrieked. Standing just inside the back door, a smudge of grease on her cheek, she had a jack handle held aloft, ready to crown somebody.

Holt stopped short. Shakily he lowered his gun. It would have been so easy to misjudge, to snap off a shot that would have gouged a bloody hole through her soft flesh.

She took a step nearer, examining him. "You're all right?"

"No, I'm not all right. I've got the shakes thinking I could have killed you. Of all the dumb stunts . . ."

He took the jack handle from her and laid it on the drainboard. The absurd smear of grease was poor make-up for Burgess's handsome features. Moistening a piece of paper towelling, he went back, held her face steady with his left hand, and wiped the grease from her cheeks.

When he'd finished, he still held her cheeks in his hand. The pressure caused her lips to pout and swell. Suddenly he wanted to kiss her.

Burgess stood quiet, her dark eyes fixed on him, breathing a fraction too fast from her dash into the house.

Holt's heartbeat speeded. Of a sudden he ached to strain all the softness of her up against him; to cut loose the tensions built up by this past week's suspense.

He fought the impulse down. He wasn't going to chance any move that would evoke another dead-fish reaction from her.

Burgess's heavy breathing swelled her breasts against the front of her sports dress. Heat built in Holt. Angrily, he commanded his feet to step back from that cold-blooded body.

173

They didn't move. Then, while he watched, Burgess's pupils dilated. Averting her face, she looked at the floor.

Holt's fingers touched her waist. Unresisting, she let herself be pulled in.

He kissed her.

Her lips compressed. Her body stiffened. Taking her face in his hands, Holt turned it up and tightened his fingers until her lips were forced to open.

Burgess's eyes became cool, removed: the old familiar story of temptation, then rejection. Angrily, Holt kissed her upper lip, strained her body to his, fastened his mouth on her lower lip in a rough caress.

For an instant, she went board-stiff. Then, all at once, her lips lost their rigidity, her body relaxed. But Holt still felt as though he were holding a frightened little animal that would dart away at any sudden gesture.

Burgess's eyes closed. Holding her just as she was, Holt gradually increased the intensity of his kisses, moving his lips down to the little hollow where her neck began.

As if it were a signal, Burgess's arms went around his neck. When he returned his lips to hers, her mouth met his in warm response, and it was she who first opened her lips in invitation. Her tongue was a warm, darting rapier. Her breasts pressed hard against his chest. Her body, soft yet firm, met his.

Then, quivering, she pulled back. Afraid she might take flight, Holt resisted the urge to snatch her up and carry her into the front room. Instead, standing where she had let him take her in his arms, he zipped open the back of her sports dress and caressed her back, gradually moving his hand down to the soft round spot above her hips.

Her eyes remained closed. She ceased to kiss him. Her body was quiet, tense, as her dress came off over her shoulders.

174

Holt kissed her around her armpits and unhooked her bra. Her breasts were already pointed little mounts. He kissed them tenderly.

Suddenly Burgess seized his shirt, pulled up fiercely, and crushed her naked breasts against his bare chest. Her breathing came sharp and rapid.

In seconds, they lay on the living room couch.

Yet even as he took her and revelled in the taking, Holt found himself watching her face, gauging her movements, looking for any of the signs of feigned passion he had learned to detect in Trix.

But Burgess obviously knew nothing of his detached observations. Her eyes shut, her breathing short and quick, she gave herself fully to the ecstasy of the moment.

Holt was not sure how long he stayed stretched comfortably on the sofa, eyes closed. Burgess lay on one side, her back lightly touching him. He assumed she was sharing the moment of pleasant languor.

Had he been stupid in so long believing the myth of Burgess's frigidity or smart in finally sensing the passion smoldering beneath her cold exterior?

Turning, he pulled her onto her back, admired her full, firm breasts and bent to kiss them.

Burgess snatched herself away, turned on her stomach and hid her face against the couch.

"I want my clothes, Holt," she snapped.

Her sharp tone slashed away his pleasant content. Bewildered, he leaned up on an elbow and scrutinized the little of her face that was visible.

She didn't wait for him to collect himself. Grabbing one of the large pillows off the floor, she covered herself as best she could and ran into the kitchen. The bolt snapped.

Sighing, Holt hauled himself up on the couch. A moment

before he'd felt the flow of spirits in his arteries. Now his muscles dragged at the effort of dressing.

Burgess's heels clicked back and forth on the kitchen floor. The water in the sink ran briefly. If she was washing away tears, getting ready to be brave about something she deplored, he was going to feel like hell. But he made himself go rap on the door.

The bolt shot back promptly. Burgess looked ready for the courts in her cotton sports dress and tennis sneakers, with her black hair snugged down by a white bandeau. Incredibly, she was smiling.

"Burgess," Holt began, "I'm sorry . . ."

Burgess's smile died. Turning, she walked to the drain board and leaned against it. "That sort of spoils it," she jerked out. "If you've got guilt feelings, why not save the weeping and wailing for Connie?"

"Now wait a minute." Holt perched on the kitchen table and ran a hand over his close-cropped hair. "You bit my head off and came flouncing in here like you were all upset."

"Am I supposed to get accustomed to you gawking at me naked . . ." Burgess snapped her fingers, ". . . just like that?"

Holt shook his head. "I give up on you, Burgess. Ever since I've known you, you've cold-shouldered any man who looked at you, especially me."

"Well, now," Burgess replied, "as to other men, not many eligibles stick around the small towns. As for you . . ."

Burgess paused, her eyes narrowed. "Just what were you offering me, Holt?"

"Why . . . why . . ." Holt stammered, "I . . ."

Burgess pushed away from the drain board and stood in the middle of the kitchen. "I'll tell you what you had to offer. Good old Burgess could sit on the sidelines during most of the games. Then maybe, once in a while, if the Holt-Connie combination wasn't working, you'd beckon to the bench and let me play for a little while."

Holt felt a warmth in his face. But Burgess wasn't being wholly fair. "Now just hold up," he said. "You've acted like that since before Connie and I got serious. Why the chill back then?"

"You were fated for her. The affluent of a small town marry the affluent of a small town." Burgess gave a short, bitter laugh. "I played games in high school with a football hero type. But as soon as the rules allowed him to marry, he married the banker's daughter."

Holt felt himself flush. "Now, wait . . ."

Abruptly, Burgess was smiling again. She came across the room and kissed him gently on the cheek. "You fancy yourself a wild Indian. Actually you're a fine man . . . tonight was my doing, not yours. But now, if I stayed around you, . . . well, we've gotten all the good there can be in this sort of thing."

"Wait a minute!" Holt got up off the table. "What do you mean, 'if you stayed'?"

Burgess crossed to the back door and gestured for him not to follow. "Me a loose woman? You an unfaithful husband? That wouldn't be any good."

Opening the door, she paused, then smiled brightly. "I believe two weeks' notice is customary. But I can leave any time you find yourself a new secretary."

Chapter 17

Friday morning at seven-fifteen, Holt opened his eyes and stretched. A pleasant languor told him that long habit, not his recent tensions, had awakened him.

He stretched wider, tightening his muscles, enjoying the sensation. Best night's sleep he'd had in weeks. He could thank Burgess for that.

Remembering the evening before, he assured himself he must be the world's prize dope when it came to women. First, he'd fallen for Trix's passion playacting. Then he'd mistaken Burgess's efficiency and aloofness for sexlessness.

Burgess! Seizing a pillow, he pulled it on top of him and crushed it against his chest, imagining Burgess's naked body there in his embrace. The thought dissipated his languor and sent waves of voluptuous sensation flooding through his body.

The telephone on the night stand interrupted with a "bri-i-ing". Somehow he was sure it was Burgess. He flipped the receiver off the hook and announced gaily, "We're going to have to come up with a better idea than your leaving."

"Leaving?" Connie's voice sharpened. "Who did you think this was, Holt?"

Connie! After a week's absence, he hadn't even called her last night. And he remembered their last conversation before he left town . . . Connie distraught and himself unyielding.

He smiled into the phone. "Been missing you, gal. How about coming down for a drink before dinner?"

"You didn't answer . . . nevermind. I've got a better idea. You've got to lunch somewhere. Bring your suit. We'll take a swim and have sandwiches."

Holt considered. He couldn't do anything about Adelaide's will until he heard from Fox. Fox would no doubt drive to Pinewood this morning. He couldn't hope to hear from the gambler until after lunch. It would be trying to hang around an office with damned little other business.

"Ho-o-olt," Connie's drawl held out allurement. "I haven't seen you in a week."

"A swim sounds like a great idea," he decided aloud. "See you about noon."

Hanging up, he lay back on the bed, folded his hands under his head and stared at the ceiling.

A minute ago in his mind he'd been crushing Burgess's naked body to his chest. Now he was thinking of Connie's sexy voice and their romping about in swim suits. Judas! It was high time he analyzed what his true feelings were.

He was, he assured himself, too mature, too seasoned for what was called young love. And he certainly was beyond mistaking every good hop in the hay for any kind of love at all.

Physically, both girls were beauties. Both excited his desire. And he didn't question the passion that Connie so carefully controlled would equal Burgess's."

Mentally, Connie had the good schools and the degree, but Burgess would never bore a man with shallowness.

Socially, Connie belonged to the inner clique. Burgess would always be asked to the larger parties.

Financially, Burgess supported herself. Connie's father could still make a comeback, and his bank was a great little feeder for law business.

Morally, . . . well, Burgess had made no bones about her high school affair. And while he didn't belong to the cult of the maidenhead, it *was* a point of comparison.

Did his rambling thoughts boil down to Burgess's succinct "the affluent of a small town marry the affluent of a small town"?

Certainly Burgess expected it to happen so again.

A steady "whir-r-r" intruded on his thoughts. He pulled himself up and went to the window. Ray, the yardman, was marching back and forth across the front lawn, giving it his regular Friday trim. That furnished the answer to one problem. Holt called down and made a deal for a ride to Tyler to get his car. Then he went to the kitchen to stuff down a bowl of the stuff plugged as crispy, crunchy, cold cereal.

A few minutes after noon, Holt drove his station wagon up the curving drive that climbed to the Townsend mansion. Leaving the vehicle on the parking apron in the rear, he ducked through the zigzag opening in the bamboo fence that screened the pool, looked around and called, "Hey! Anybody here?"

Connie stuck her head out of the door to the women's dressing room.

"I'm changing," she announced. "Get ready and we'll take a dip first."

Suit in hand, Holt circled the pool and walked under the thatched roof of the summer house into the men's dressing room. From behind the flimsy partition that separated it from the room where Connie was changing came the sound of sandals clicking back and forth on the cement floor.

The awareness of Connie so near titillated his imagination. As he began to strip, he stared at the dividing

181

wall and let his mind become a penny peep-show, revolving pictures of Connie in the process of changing clothes.

"Holt, I can't make up my mind which suit to wear." Connie's normal conversational tone carried as though there were no partition. "Would it shock you if I wore the new bikini I got for sunning?"

Holt stopped his mental kinetograph on a single picture — Connie standing there in nothing but her sandals, a bathing suit in each hand. "Wear it!" he commanded.

"I don't know if I have the nerve — out in broad daylight with someone around."

Holt chuckled. "With that built-up, I'll blow a gasket if you don't."

"Well . . . all right."

The pictures inside Holt's head grew even more vivid. Quickly, he tugged on his bathing trunks, went out into the summer house, and settled on a bamboo chaise lounge in the path of the air flow from an evaporative cooler.

The thick thatched roof provided a deep shade that held the restful coolness. But, eager for a look at Connie, Holt didn't lean back or relax.

Then Connie came out — covered in a bulky terry cloth robe that concealed her curves in a shapeless sack.

Holt made a wry face. "That's a hell of a disappointment," he observed.

"I can't imagine what you're talking about." Connie paused to give him a peck on the cheek, then crossed to the bar that faced the dressing rooms. "What'll you have to drink?"

Holt thought about having to meet Fox, and the fast action that would be necessary to corral a witness for Monday's hearing. "No liquor," he replied. "I've got work to do."

Connie's lips drew into a pout. "I'm not going to drink

by myself. And I need something if I'm going to get up the nerve to take this robe off."

Holt smiled in spite of himself. "You do know how to sell a guy, don't you? — Okay, a light scotch and soda." He crossed to the bar and perched on one of the tall stools.

Connie pushed a dark brown drink across the counter. Holt lifted an eyebrow and held the glass up for examination. Then he glanced at the drink Connie brought with her as she came around the bar and sat beside him. It looked equally potent.

They drank together. Over his glass, Holt studied Connie.

For a moment, when she'd given him the liberally laced drink, he'd wondered if she was softening him up for another proposition of her father's.

But, seeing what she'd mixed for herself, he decided she only wanted to make sure he didn't dash off to the office and cut short this moment of relaxation.

That was like Connie. Life with her would be fun. She'd always be planning a party or a vacation. And that, Holt knew, would be good for a man too inclined to drive himself.

He took another sip of his drink. Already the alcohol had dulled the edge of his anxiety about Monday's hearing ... and erased his momentary uncertainty as to Connie's motives.

Now Connie lifted a foot and rested it on the rail of her chair. The terry cloth robe parted, revealing a naked brown thigh. "A penny for your thoughts," she said.

Holt eyed the shapely curve and smiled. "I was thinking about us. If I can just get into the saddle in Adelaide's estate, we'll be all set."

"You're the one that has to have it made before we marry." Connie's eyes swept the patio, the pool, and the roof of the mansion just visible over the bamboo fence. "I think it's all this that makes you so money conscious."

183

"Oh?" Again Holt studied her. "Up till now you haven't argued against the idea that I ought to be able to support you."

"And look like I was trying to trap you in a hurry? You bet I haven't!" Connie took a long sip of her drink and carried it with her to the chaise lounge. Resting against the chair's back, she crossed her legs in front of her and let the bottom part of her robe fall open.

Glass in hand, Holt followed and lifted her legs so he could sit beside her.

Connie took another sip. Holt looked closely to see if she showed any signs of feeling the drink. He was aware of the warmth of the alcohol running through his own body and knew it was affecting him more because his system didn't expect it at this time of day.

With her free hand, Connie flipped the edge of her robe over her legs. "I'd probably have done a lot of things differently if I hadn't wanted to be sure I didn't do one damn thing the same as that hussy that hooked you first."

"Forget Trix! Be yourself." Annoyed, Holt stared out over the pool. "Every time you come around me, you cram yourself into that damned girdle, and we have to act as skittish as a couple of experimenting pubescents. All because Trix was a tramp. Is she going to run our lives?"

Connie said nothing. Holding her glass to her lips, she looked over the top, her hazel eyes somber. Then the little flecks of green began to dance.

"O-o-o-ooh, grumpy!" She reached up and put her hands around his neck and pulled his head down for a kiss.

"Damned right I'm grumpy!" Holt transferred his drink to his left hand and slid his right under Connie's robe. He squeezed her calf, then moved his palm up the under side of her leg to the knee and lightly stroked the soft hollow there.

Connie took the last sip of her drink and set it on the

184

floor with an air of finality. Then she pressed the wet, cold palm that had held the glass against the inside of Holt's thigh. He started.

She giggled in return, but her open hand remained. He felt her palm warm gradually, and the pulse inside her hand throbbed gently against his flesh. A glow started at the spot where her hand rested in that casual, intimate touch.

Connie drew her left leg toward her, raising it a few inches off the couch. Spreading his fingers, Holt let them play along the under side of her thigh as he moved his hand upward until he could feel the cleft where the round swell of her hips began.

Her skin was smooth, firm, unbelievably warm.

He squeezed the springy flesh of her hip, feeling the narrow band of cloth. "I like your bikini even without seeing it," he said. "It's a sensible garment. You can't have a girdle hidden under it."

"I'm not sure that's a good idea," Connie murmured. "Someone around here's getting pretty familiar."

Leaning forward, he kissed her. Connie's lips responded, provacatively active. She moved her hand along his thigh. He quivered.

Then, releasing her, he drew back.

Connie raised an eyebrow inquiringly.

"Got to watch my blood pressure," Holt said. "You wouldn't be wearing that rig if you didn't have Christine about to barge in with sandwiches."

"It's Christine's day off."

"And your dad at the bank? What is this, a switch?" Holt leaned forward again, gave the lobe of Connie's ear a tender bite and brushed his lips along her neck to the little hollow made by her collar bone.

Connie wriggled away. "Now don't get ideas. If I were sure you knew I'm a good girl, you might manage to get me to be a bad one. But you obviously don't."

Her words pressed a button in Holt. Suddenly serious, he looked her squarely in the face. "But I obviously do," he corrected. "Connie, after the deal Trix handed me, you can bet that was the first thing I had to believe about you before I asked you to marry me."

Connie gave him a long, serious, very sober look. "I think it's time I accepted that, Holt," she said. "Let's leave it, that, starting now, I no longer think I have to prove something to you."

Then she laughed, pulled her legs from beside him, flipped them over his head and to the floor. Standing, she smiled, "I should have known I'd lose an argument with a lawyer. I'm going to cool off."

With a fluid motion, she slipped out of her robe and threw it across the back of the chaise lounge. Holt drew in a sharp breath.

For a moment he saw only her naked brown body, dark against the delicate white face that Connie kept protected from freckles. Then he made out the negligible bikini, matched to the bronze of her flesh and molded into the shape of small, firm breasts and full, promising hips.

Connie crossed to a round bamboo table and picked up a bathing cap. She pulled the cap over her chestnut hair and kicked off her sandals.

Her nearly naked body, held proudly, tantalized Holt. Pushing up off the couch, he started for her.

Connie laughed, ran to the side of the pool, and made a clean, deep dive. Without checking his stride, Holt threw himself in after her, shooting across the surface of the water, Then, jackknifing, he did a scissors and plunged downward.

Using a flutter kick, Connie spurted through the water. Holt made a grab, missed her, and got the end of one of the knots that held the flimsy band around her waist. It came loose in his hand.

Connie arched her back, stroked vigorously, and took off at a right angle. With less grace, Holt pulled himself around with the strength of his arms and swam after her. Watching her legs flutter back and forth, the frog-like motion of his breast stroke and scissor kick felt awkward.

Connie reached the edge of the pool and surfaced. Close behind, Holt shot up beside her. Then, catching the pool's rim with one hand, he turned to face her.

Connie laughed. She was supporting herself with both hands, facing outward from the pool.

Then, in the midst of her mirth, her eyes widened suddenly. Holt followed her stare.

Old man Townsend had appeared at the entrance to the patio. Blinking against the sunlight, he swiveled his big beak nose left and right.

"Connie," he called. "You here, Connie?"

Hastily Holt wound the G-string into a small wad and concealed it in his fist. Connie, in her turn, hugged the side of the pool, only her head above water.

"What is it, Dad?" she snapped.

Townsend started, then peered down. The old boy looked pale and shaky. Holt almost felt sorry for him even though he shared Connie's annoyance.

"I . . . I wondered if you'd had a chance to talk to Holt," Townsend quavered, his voice hoarse.

Connie's nostrils flared. She inhaled-exhaled impatiently. "Dad, if you'd just give me a chance . . . No, I haven't."

Holt saw the banker's watery, pale blue eyes focus on him.

"Holt," Townsend implored, "I've got to talk to you —" But Connie cut in:

"Dad, *please!* For heaven's sake, leave it to me!"

Townsend hesitated, shuffled from one foot to another.

Whatever was bothering the old man, he really had the fidgets.

"Dad," Connie said in a more patient tone, "go on back to the bank. I'll call you."

Looking defeated, Townsend turned and went out.

Wordlessly Holt handed over the bottom half of Connie's bikini. She knotted it about her carelessly, got out of the pool, and pulled on the terry cloth robe. The gaiety of a moment before was gone.

Holt joined Connie. Toweling himself, he asked, "What was all that about?"

Connie pulled her bathing cap off, threw if on the table, and slumped into one of the straight chairs. "Dammit, Holt, now you're going to think I was softening you up, and I don't blame you."

"Maybe I won't blame you. Just tell me what's got him so shaken up." Holt circled the table, sat down facing her and waited.

Connie made a small gesture with one hand, palm up. "It's the same thing I talked to you about. Dad needs money. Reg want to help. You've got Reg blocked."

Holt tried to keep the impatience out of his voice. "I told your dad I'd arrange a loan for him. I can handle the directors as soon as I'm voting Adelaide's stock."

"How soon will that be?"

"Monday, I hope." Holt pushed back in his chair and crossed his legs. "Look, Connie, stop letting him upset you. I told you there's nothing so terrible his creditors can do."

"Holt, you said yourself that if either side appeals, the case could go on and on. Dad's got to have a quick way to settle everything."

"I've heard it twenty times — sell Adelaide's Breads."

"But, Holt, there's a fortune in it for us. We can marry, go anywhere."

188

"That part's new." Holt cocked an eyebrow. "How do I come into this fortune?"

Connie leaned forward. The terry cloth robe parted, revealing her slim, near-naked body. But she was all business now.

"Reg owes Kane a fourth of the estate as a fee now. But he has to give him another fourth if you carry a contest through the courts. Reg will give that fourth to us . . . to you . . . if you forget about the will."

"No dice."

"But Holt," Connie protested, "we could . . ."

Holt shook his head firmly. "It's not as good as having the two best clients in town in my hip pocket — and being chairman of the board of a bank and a million dollar corporation."

There was no reason to mention Miss Phoebe, or the charities that would come into Adelaide's estate if Reg died childless, or his own aversion to throwing a game. These matters, Holt assured himself, were not the considerations that were shaping his decision.

Connie sat back in her chair and bit her lower lip. Then she looked Holt squarely in the face. "You listen to me, Holt. I couldn't marry you if you let anything happen to Dad."

"Nothing's going to happen to him. I told you —"

"No, Holt!" Connie's hand cut off his words. Tears welled in her eyes, rolled down her cheeks.

For a long moment, then, she didn't speak. When she finally went on, her voice was tight and choked.

"Something awful's going to happen to him, Holt," she whispered. "Something — you don't know how awful."

Again, she halted; again, regained control:

"Because — if the bank examiners walk in with things like they are right now — well, my father's going to the penitentiary!"

189

Chapter 18

The dressing room was steamy hot when Holt reentered. Irritably, he threw his towel at the basket in the corner, and yanked off his bathing trunks. Damn old man Townsend, anyway! How the hell could a man smart enough to head a bank be stupid enough to get in a spot where he faced an embezzling rap?

Near the base of the room's outer wall a rectangle of wood had been cut out and replaced. That was where Connie had planned to put air-conditioning, and doting daddy must have let her go ahead at the very time he was losing his shirt! But there was no use rehashing past mistakes. The facts remained the same, and you had to deal with them, no matter how infuriated it made you.

The sound of soft, steady sobbing came through the partition from the room where Connie was changing. Snatching up his underwear, Holt jerked it on. Apparently he'd been elected Most Unreasonable Brute. Because he was blocking the sale of Adelaide's Breads — and the money Reg would get for his stock was the only possible source for the quick cash needed to save Connie's dad and Reg. And neither hornet's nest could await the outcome of a protracted will contest.

Yet, would there necessarily be a long contest? Holt

paused in his dressing. Suppose he dug up one of the phony witnesses and probated Adelaide's will. Would Kane appeal? Hell, no! He'd be too busy trying to hush the whole thing up.

And right this minute Fox might have a lead to those witnesses!

An extension telephone sat on the bar outside. Hastily, Holt stuffed his shirt into his trousers. Then, unable to contain his impatience, ignoring sox, shoes, coat and tie, he trotted out to the phone in his bare feet and dialed the office.

Burgess sounded irritated. "Holt, I've tried to track you down all over town. Where have you been?"

Holt gave the telephone an unhappy look. "Have you heard from Fox?" he countered.

"That's why I needed you. He's called a half dozen times. The last time just a few minutes ago."

"What'd he say?"

"I'll give you an exact quote. He said, 'Young Bailey's at the clinic; Kane's probably at the sheriff's; and I damn sure can't hang around any longer. Now where the hell's that stupid jerk you work for?' "

Holt grimaced. He deserved that for not letting Burgess know he was at Connie's.

"Where is Fox now?" he demanded.

"I thought you must have gone to Tyler to get your car. He said he'd catch you there or on the road. He's driving a black Cadillac and told me to let you know to look out for it if you called in."

"I'm on my way!" Holt started to hang up.

Burgess's sharp "wait a minute" stopped him.

"What else?" Holt asked impatiently.

"Mr. Oates, that lawyer in Hilma, called. Said it was urgent you get the message that Manuel flashed a roll of bills around his buddies and then took off for parts unknown."

"What's he doing to find him?"

"Nothing, I guess. He said to tell you if Manuel had gone to Mexico, an army of private detective couldn't find him by Monday."

Putting the phone back in its cradle, Holt stared tight-lipped across the pool. Now he had nothing to back up the improbable story of how Adelaide had executed her will. He'd get no delay from Woodruff. For a second he considered the fiasco Monday was going to be if he didn't turn up a witness to Adelaide's will. Then he dashed back to the dressing room.

Shoe strings tangled, and tie refused to knot. But in sixty seconds he rushed out again. Connie was coming from the women's room. She'd changed to a modest white linen dress.

Her tears had left her eyes red-rimmed. "I don't suppose you've had any second thoughts," she said in a small, sad voice.

"I've had some second thoughts." Holt eyed Connie's provacative curves and the empty highball glasses beside the chaise lounge. He didn't know what motive or mixture of motives had prevailed with Connie, but he did know that only Townsend's interruption had kept them from winding up on that lounge. He wouldn't be human if he hadn't had second thoughts!

Connie came nearer. "What are your second thoughts, Holt?"

"I think that every time we talk, either Reg or your Dad has a new reason for me to throw in the towel. My second thought is that you better tell them it'll be faster and surer for Reg to bring in one of his slippery witnesses so I can probate Adelaide's will. Then, if he'll tell Kane to forget any appeal, in nothing flat I'll buy Reg's stock for the estate at enough to settle with Fox and cover for your Dad."

Connie shook her head. "Kane wouldn't let Reg give in,"

she said.

Holt took her by the shoulders and propelled her ahead of him through the zigzag opening in the bamboo fence.

"If you want to get all this over with, you better get on the phone and sell Reg." He boosted her toward the house and gave her behind the kind of spank he'd use to encourage a fellow footballer. "Because," he asserted, "I won't give in either."

The speed at which Holt took the curving Townsend drive swerved his station wagon from side to side. He kept his foot heavy on the throttle until he reached the Tyler highway and then he floor-boarded it. His speed wouldn't allow any quick stops, and he strained eyes and nerves to anticipate any build-up of traffic ahead.

A few miles out of Pinewood stood the only hill high enough to lay claim to the name of mountain.

As Holt passed Mountain Look-out Park, he eased back on the throttle. Just over the crest of the hill, a straight, steep descent led to a narrow, antiquated bridge edged with sturdy stone walls . . . a death trap for speeders in modern, wide cars. Knowing the danger, Holt scanned the slope.

Trouble. A jam of cars crowded about the bridge. Then came the distant screeching of a siren. In his rear-view mirrow, Holt saw flashing red lights climbing the road behind. He pulled over and stopped by one of the several "Narrow Bridge" signs that lined the highway.

"Damn," he grumbled and began to debate making a detour. But Fox had said to watch for him on the road.

Then George White's ambulance-hearse limousine screamed past. At the foot of the hill, tiny uniformed figures seemed to have the cars moving in alternating one-way columns.

That decided him. Holt let his car coast forward. Soon he could see what obstructed the right-hand lane. A large, black sedan had impaled itself on the stone wall that edged the bridge.

Holt's stomach tightened with foreboding. The wrecked car had been headed for Tyler, as was Fox. Holt parked and began to walk to the bridge; but his need to know spurred him into a trot.

The car that had split itself on the bridge's side was a black Cadillac. A highway patrolman stood by it. Dreading the answer, Holt asked, "Were they . . . is anybody alive?"

The patrolman glanced at the tangled wreck that the bridge had cleaved almost in half. "You've got to be kidding," he observed and turned toward where George and Joe White were loading two bodies on stretchers.

Fox was dead, Holt was miserably sure. But he had to make certain that it was the gambler who'd died in the wreck.

He touched the patrolman's arm. "I think I may know the men. Could I see . . ."

The officer regarded him with new interest. "We like to get an actual identification." He gestured with a wallet he had in his hand. "Sometimes these things are packed with lies." He led the way to the stretchers.

George White nodded. "Hi, Holt," he said.

Holt returned the nod. "Hi, George . . . Joe."

"This man wants to take a look," the patrolman said.

George White made a gesture of dismissal toward one stretcher. "You couldn't tell a thing from that mess, Holt." Turning, he flipped back the sheet covering the other body. "This head's okay."

Holt choked back a feeling of nausea and filled his lungs with fresh air.

It was Fox. In death, the gambler's waxy face looked like that of a vulture. Conscious charm no longer concealed the greedy lines.

Holt wondered how many mourners such a character would have. At least he had one person to regret his death. Holt did — for his own greedy reason. Now he had no lead on the witnesses to Adelaide's will — no hope of probating it on Monday. Unless — he remembered how George White had stripped Adelaide's body of all personal effects.

Looking up, Holt asked, "He was supposed to have an address for me, George. Did you find any kind of memo?"

George White shook his head. "Not a scrap of any kind."

Holt turned and spoke to the highway patrolman. "His name's Arthur Fox. Comes from Dallas. He lists as a lawyer and practices as a gambler."

"That first part checks with his license. Thanks for the help." Before Holt could repeat his question, the patrolman gestured with the wallet he held. "I've already combed through this. There's no name or address but Fox's."

Bleakly, Holt turned away from the body. As things stood, he couldn't probate Adelaide's will. And Judge Woodruff had made it amply clear that in such event he would put Reg in as administrator and okay the sale of Adelaide's plant.

Holt balled his fists. He should have gone ahead and himself wrung the truth out of Reg. Now Kane would have that precious young man under close guard until Monday and well coached for questions then.

The Whites carried the first stretcher to the hearse and hoisted it in. The crowd of curious farmers and travelers began to break up.

Holt gave the scene a final, miserable glance and started for his car. A "hey" from the patrolman stopped him.

"You sure this Fox was a gambler . . . I mean a professional one?" the officer demanded.

Holt nodded. "I'm sure. Why?"

"Could be we've got one of those gang killings. There're

no skid marks, and the left front fender's scraped. I had it figured that some damn fool tried to pass, wedged them into the wall, then panicked and ran."

Holt felt a prickly sensation at the back of his neck. He started to say something, but checked himself. He didn't want to volunteer anything that would get him involved in answering questions.

But, as he trudged back to his car, he admitted to himself that through the years he had misjudged Kane. He'd thought of him as a theatrical shyster.

But what a perfect scheme Kane had come up with to disqualify Adelaide's will even as she was pacified with the thought that she'd left her affairs as she wanted them.

How cleverly he'd accomplished Adelaide's death.

How quickly he'd spirited Manuel away.

And now . . . how had Kane without the least delay managed Fox's death and the destruction of whatever information Reg had supplied?

Yes, Holt had misjudged him.

Kane was a diabolical genius!

In comparison, Holt felt angelically inept. He made a U-turn and drove slowly in the direction of Pinewood. A confused flow of thoughts and emotions pounded his brain. Logic told him he was licked. Manuel had disappeared. Any possible lead to the missing witnesses had died with Fox.

Only Kane and Reg remained to tell what happened at the execution of Adelaide's will, and they'd unhesitatingly perjure themselves.

Holt gritted his teeth. He hated to quit. At Mountain Look-out Park, he pulled off the road and parked. He needed somehow to sort the conflicting ideas and feelings tugging at him.

Below him, the massive red courthouse towered above the rest of Pinewood.

To the left, the Townsend's English manor house was visible atop its terraced hill. Holt pursed his lips. What was holding him? He ought to get himself over there and tell Connie to grab Reg's offer of a fourth of the estate. Don't be a damned fool, he told himself. Take it. Take Connie. Take yourself out of the game.

On the right, wisps of smoke curled up from the tall smokestacks that topped Adelaide's plant. So all right. It would be tough on the men and their families when the bakery was rolled up. Tough on a lot of others, too. But that was life.

Glancing down, Holt saw his whitened knuckles and realized he was trying to strangle the steering wheel.

But what could he do? What could all of them, Adelaide included, expect him to do when he hadn't a scrap of evidence . . . unless you counted the perjury he'd get from Kane and Reg.

Perjury from Kane and Reg . . . suddenly he felt a quickened heart beat, a feeling of warmth just under the skin, a familiar tingling all through his being.

What else could he do? Holt gritted his teeth. He could slug back, that's what! He'd never stood in the middle of a football field wringing his hands and wondering what to do after getting mousetrapped!

If Kane liked theatrics, he'd give him theatrics. Two could play at theatrics. Two could play at setting traps . . . and the bait would be perjury!

Then Holt shook his head. Woodruff would see him fined, jailed, disbarred. You didn't run risks like that for a dead client and men you hardly knew.

All at once, the smoke coming from Adelaide's plant died out. Holt drew in a sharp breath. How quickly the bakery began to look lifeless. Then a puff came from the tall chimneys, and again a steady cloud curled upward. Holt breathed deeply. The engineer must have been adjusting the furnace. Holt felt abashed at his sudden surge of relief.

Almost before he realized he'd made a final decision, he started the station wagon and turned it toward Dallas.

Chapter 19

On Monday morning, Holt drove his station wagon east along the Dallas highway. Ahead, to the right, the Pinewood exit came into view. Slowing, Holt turned for a final inspection of Theodore Calhoun.

He hardly recognized him as the man from the magic shop . . . Abe Lincoln's double, who'd opened Adelaide's safe.

Shorn of his exaggerated sideburns and theatrical look, Calhoun appeared a successful professional man — blue business suit, white broadcloth shirt, maroon tie of elegant simplicity.

With a nod of approval, Holt turned back to watching the road. "You know your lines now?"

"Of course. I've just got a bit part."

Holt twisted the rear view mirror so he could see and reassured himself that Oliver Calhoun was his twin's duplicate in every respect. "You all set, Oliver?"

Oliver Calhoun snorted. "All set? Good Lord, all I've got is a walk-on."

Now a sign appeared: "City Limits. Pinewood, Pop.: 4,957. Water Supply Approved."

Holt glanced at his wristwatch. Eight fifteen. Exactly on time.

"Theodore, you got a dime to get into the john?" he questioned.

"Holt, you've given me three dimes for the can already." Theodore chuckled. "I shall await Oliver's call concealed in the most humiliating dressing room ever assigned me. Just don't you blow up."

Holt cocked an eyebrow. "If I do, you can wire your agent you won't be 'at liberty' for some time."

Then he pulled his car over to the curb and again checked his watch. Eight seventeen. Theodore would have just the right amount of time to walk to the courthouse.

After a cautious look up and down the street, Theodore gave a half salute with crossed fingers and slipped out of the car.

At the courthouse, Holt joined the line of automobiles circling the square. Knots of men spotted the courthouse lawn.

"We've got a good house," Oliver Calhoun observed.

Taking a closer look, Holt recognized a number of the hands from Adelaide's plant. Burgess must have spread the word that today's hearing would tell the story on whether the plant stayed open. And with sure trouper instinct, Oliver had sensed that this mob was out for the dramatics.

Butterflies fluttered lightly in Holt's stomach. If only these poor bastards' jobs didn't depend on what he did in the next hour!

Oliver obviously felt no such misgivings. His face, framed in the rear view mirrow, was positively glowing.

"It's a damned shame I can't turn the lead role over to you," Holt said dryly.

But it was nice that the Calhouns were getting such a kick out of this thing. Because what they'd get would be a kick in the pants if the screwball plan misfired.

Early arrivers had taken every parking place around the

square. Suddenly impatient, Holt wrenched his station wagon out of the slowly circling line of cars.

The nearest open spot turned out to be a surprising three blocks off the square. Holt dragged his briefcase and an ancient portable typewriter out of the back of the station wagon and headed toward the courthouse. Following, Oliver Calhoun momentarily matched strides, then broke into a trot. "Hey," he protested, "I thought curtain time was nine o'clock."

Forcing himself to slow his pace, Holt gave his companion a crooked grin. "It is. I just want to be sure there's no slip-up in setting the stage for our little production."

Side by side, they crossed the courthouse lawn. Hands waved from clumps of men. Holt nodded acknowledgment but kept going. Letting himself get delayed wouldn't help the cause.

At the foot of the courthouse steps, the crowd was so thick as to block passage. Waiting for a path to open, Holt glanced up at the windows of Judge Woodruff's courtroom. The backs of men showing there indicated that the walls were already lined with spectators. Burgess had seen to it that the judge would look out at a mob of interested voters.

Still higher, one of the red granite gargoyles grinned down from the roof as though immensely amused.

Now an older man with cotton curly hair and flour still whitening his blue work pants took a half step forward. "We'll root for you from here, Mr. Lawson. The fellows up there are going to give us the word."

He raised two fingers in a V-for-victory sign. "This is if you win." Then he drew a finger across his throat in a slitting motion. "This is for us if Kane gets the nod." He laughed nervously and stepped back.

Lips tight, Holt nodded and followed Oliver up the

packed stairs. Amazing, the speed and accuracy of a small-town grapevine. The whole population knew the score.

On the third floor, a cluster of men and women in front of the glass-paned courtroom door blocked the entrance. Beckoning for Oliver to follow, Holt led the way further along the corridor to the court clerk's office.

From the clerk's inner door, Holt could look out over the courtroom. Older men and women folk were squeezed together on every bench. With small-town politeness, the able-bodied had abandoned the seats and now lined the walls two and three deep.

Oliver Calhoun stood on tip-toe and looked over Holt's shoulder. "Standing room only!" he exclaimed. "This show's ready for Broadway!"

"It's got a sure-fire formula," Holt agreed. "Nero used to fill the Colosseum when folks knew somebody'd get slaughtered." Then, moving aside a step, he surveyed the courtroom's business area.

Frail little Mr. Meade, court bailiff, patrolled the railing that blocked off the spectators. Sitting by themselves at the counsel table, Burgess and Miss Phoebe had their heads close together. Next to Burgess's dark sheen, Miss Phoebe's fine, white hair looked like a halo surrounding her round kindly face. Burgess had Miss Phoebe dressed in a black, old-fashioned dress. No complexion.

Holt grunted his satisfaction. No need to give Miss Phoebe any lines. Just sitting there, she'd remind Judge Woodruff that Reg had already tried to throw her out of her home once, and would be free to finish the job if Adelaide's will wasn't probated.

The crowd was a somewhat different story from a stadium full of football nuts. These people hadn't picked their bets. Their homes and jobs were at stake through no fault of theirs.

Burgess looked up. It was time to go. Holt wished he were about to trot out onto a football field, surrounded by teammates\and able to jog around and start tossing the ball. But he turned to Oliver.

Eyes sparkling, Oliver fidgeted like a trouper awaiting his cue in the stage's wings.

Holt took a deep breath. "Okay, buddy, let's go." Then, squaring his shoulders, he led the way out into the courtroom.

Here ceiling fans droned, pressed back into service to help the laboring air conditioner. But a louder buzzing immediately drowned out the hum of the machines as the crowd spotted Holt's entrance.

The attention thrilled and chilled him both at once. Putting a confident smile on his face, he marched to the far side of the counsel table.

Then he managed a genuine grin. As usual, Burgess had grabbed the side of the table next to the jury box. Probably she'd come an hour early to cinch it. The only catch was, Texas procedure didn't allow a jury in a county court hearing on a will. Burgess was going to feel like kicking him for forgetting to tell her.

Holt gave Miss Phoebe's shoulders a reassuring squeeze as he passed behind her, restrained himself from doing the same to Burgess, and indicated the chair nearest the judge's bench for Oliver.

The seats across the table were empty. The opposition hadn't arrived.

Settling himself between Burgess and Oliver, Holt zipped his briefcase open and made a final inspection of his troupe. On his right, Oliver: solid professional type. Farthest on his left, Miss Phoebe: sweet little chunk of goodness.

And lastly, Burgess, the acme of secretarial perfection. Her tailored, short-sleeved brown dress allowed her to look handsome but not noticeably sexy.

Now the buzzing of the crowd rose sharply. Holt looked up.

Judge Woodruff had appeared on his elevated dais. He was seated before Holt could get to his feet.

Almost in the same instant the buzzing stepped up to a stridence that set teeth on edge.

That had to be Kane.

The gray-haired giant came through the door of the clerk's office, threw the spectators a triumphant smile, and turned to the woman who followed him. Holt recognized the square jaw of Mrs. Sam Shelton.

Kane gave Mrs. Shelton his arm and, continuing to beam on one and all, led her to the empty jury box. Shelton and Townsend followed. Holt could sense still others were coming.

So this was Kane's counter to the courtroom filled with bakery employees! He was marching Pinewood's first families in front of Judge Woodruff and parking them in the shadow of the bench where it wouldn't be forgotten that the elite were for Reg's side.

Holt fiddled with the papers in his briefcase. The fact that Kane had thought to grab the empty jury box and parade his supporters to it didn't matter particularly. But the pale-eyed giant hadn't been taken unawares. And Holt's whole plan of attack depended on surprise.

The procession to the jury box continued: Townsend's cashier and vice-president. Obviously supers pulled in to fill chairs.

Turning, Holt watched Kane get the five persons he'd ushered in seated, heard him assure them it was perfectly all right to use the seats.

The sixth chair remained empty. Holt eyed it with an unhappy premonition. Sure enough, Connie appeared in the clerk's door, along with a beaming Reg.

The paper Holt held began to shake, exaggerating the angry trembling of his hands. But Connie pulled back from the arm Reg proffered and shook her head.

Unaccompanied, she walked directly toward the counsel table. The snug cut and tightly roped belt of her green dress revealed the delicate perfection of her figure. Holt thought of the delicious moments Friday at her pool . . . until old man Townsend crashed in. And he wondered if she were bringing an answer to the message he'd given her for Reg.

Connie came straight to him. Holt got up and swung his empty chair around for her, a little removed from Burgess. Then he leaned against the table where he'd screen Oliver from the opposition.

"I take it from Kane's triumphal procession that Reg won't settle for just the income he'd get under Adelaide's will."

Connie shook her head. "Kane said they'll have it all eventually . . . with no strings. And that Judge Woodruff will clear the way today for the sale and enough cash to fix things for Dad."

Holt shrugged. "I expected that."

"Kane said Reg would be a fool to give you anything." Connie's eyes widened. "Holt, what *are* you going to do?"

"Do?" Holt chuckled. "Connie, there's been a public notice posted on the courthouse door for ten days. I'm going to probate Adelaide's will."

"But . . ."

Holt raised a hand, and she dropped the matter.

Then she looked at the empty seat in the jury box next to her father. "Dad says I've got to sit there, Holt. That we've got to cooperate with Reg."

Holt snorted. "No wonder Adelaide used to browbeat him. It works." His voice began to rise with anger. "Well, if

205

you want to show the town you're taking sides against me . . ."

"I don't," Connie interrupted. "I won't." She gave his arm a squeeze and went out through the clerk's office.

Holt enjoyed watching her walk out on Kane's rooters. Connie was made of better stuff than her father. Then an annoying thought occurred to him, and he yanked his chair beneath him. It could be that she was just smarter.

Obviously no one in Kane's party questioned what the outcome of the hearing would be. Which meant that Kane had checked with his bogus witnesses, found all well, and given definite assurances of victory.

Leaving the jury box, Kane swaggered around the table, grinned scornfully at Holt and struck a majestic pose for the crowd.

Holt ignored the bit of pantomime. In fact, he welcomed Kane's approach and the necessity of fixing his thoughts on his opponent.

As he took his seat, Kane pulled the corners of his mouth down and nodded briefly. Clearly he was ready for the kill, secure in the knowledge that his witnesses were safe under wraps.

Holt acknowledged Kane's nod with a quick jerk of his head. Now the fighters had shaken hands and could come out battling.

Burgess leaned back in her chair and started to speak to Oliver Calhoun. With an abrupt back-and-fourth motion of his hand, Holt put the kibosh on that.

Now Kane's pale reptilian eyes moved to Calhoun . . . narrowed thoughtfully. Then, swiveling around to Reg, the big lawyer whispered something.

Reg leaned forward to study Calhoun a moment.

The movement caused Holt to notice a discoloration under Reg's left eye . . . a bruise almost concealed by a thick coat of powder. Holt smiled inwardly as he visualized Reg's tete-á-tete with Gino.

Reg completed his inspection of Calhoun and shrugged his shoulders.

Turning back, Kane leaned across the table and held out his hand. "I'm Matthew Kane," he said.

"Glad to know you." Oliver's cordial reply made his failure to give his own name appear an oversight.

Under the table Holt crossed his fingers and knocked on wood. He'd anticipated that feeler of Kane's when coaching Oliver in his part.

A sharp rap from the judge's bench cut Kane off from further prying.

Out beyond the railing the buzzing of the spectators went on unchecked by the gavelling. Judge Woodruff cleared his throat and swept the courtroom with his colorless, glaring eye. A sudden silence descended in the wake of his glower.

"Both sides ready in the Bailey matter?" the judge demanded.

Kane came quickly to his feet. "Your honor," he boomed, "we're ready on the application of Reginald Bailey to be appointed temporary administrator. We are further anxious to dispose of the question of the probate of Adelaide Bailey's will if Mr. Lawson is ready to proceed in that matter."

He stayed on his feet, waiting. Waiting, Holt knew, to protest the request Holt would have to make for delay on probating the will. Poised to demand Reg's immediate appointment as administrator in accordance with Judge Woodruff's commitment.

A smile tugged at the corners of Holt's mouth as he got to his feet. "We're ready on both matters, your honor," he announced cheerfully.

For a moment Kane stayed on his feet. Staring, he wiped

his open mouth with the palm of his hand. Then he seemed to remember he was still standing and abruptly sat down.

Judge Woodruff turned to Holt. "I'll hear from you first on the will matter. No need for an administrator if we probate the will. Let's get all the witnesses sworn."

Kane stood. "I have no witnesses, your Honor." He waved a hand toward the jury box. "These fine people are here only to observe, although they have a vital interest in the case."

Holt stood, also. "Nevertheless, I'll ask that Mr. Shelton and Mr. Townsend be sworn, along with Reginald Bailey." He gestured for Oliver to rise.

Reg grabbed for Kane's arm and began to whisper excitedly. A worried frown clouded his flushed face.

Kane got to his feet and faced the judge. "May I ask the purpose of swearing my client as a witness?"

"You may when he's called," Judge Woodruff said shortly and brought his good eye around to bear on the witnesses. "Stand up and raise your right hands. You, too, Mr. Bailey."

Now Holt forgot Connie, himself, and their problems. The game had started, and he only knew one way to play — with his whole heart and mind and soul. To play to win with every fibre of his being. He threw quick glances about as though he were back on the gridiron trying to see what was happening everywhere on the field.

Across the table, Reg got to his feet with obvious reluctance and raised his right hand. Holt smiled to himself. Good. He had Reg worried.

Eyes riveted on Oliver Calhoun, Kane sat chewing his lower lip. Holt nodded. Good again. Kane's suspicions were up.

Judge Woodruff ran through the oath quickly. Kane leaned forward in his chair and cupped his hand to his ear as the witnesses repeated their names. Well coached, Oliver mumbled his name so that it was drowned out by the others.

Kane's fingers began to drum on the table. In a moment he'd find another way to probe. Holt nodded his head a fraction of an inch.

On cue, Oliver leaned forward and asked in a hoarse, carrying whisper, "Okay if I slip out a minute? — Took some magnesia last night."

"Sure." Holt tried to keep his voice casual and paid no attention as Oliver pushed his way through the crowd into the hall.

Now it was time to divert Kane further. Holt faced the bench.

"Your Honor, I call Reginald Bailey to the stand."

Reg grabbed for Kane's arm. But Kane was already getting to his feet. Holt watched, gauging the state of Reg's nerves. Kane's coaching might have supplied all the answers, but it hadn't instilled any enthusiasm in Reg for giving them.

"Your Honor!" Kane bit out the words. "May I now ask the purpose of calling my client to the stand?"

Holt half-faced toward Kane. "I have to prove the testatrix was of age and of sound mind when she executed the will. Can't think of a better witness than her next of kin."

Kane took a deep breath. "Is that the only purpose you have for calling Mr. Bailey?" he demanded suspiciously.

"That's all," Holt replied.

Relief showed on Reg's face.

Kane's cruel blue eyes glittered. He grinned in scorn. "Then let's save time. I stipulate that the testatrix was of sound mind and of age when she signed her will. That these witnesses will be taken to have so testified."

It required no genius to follow Kane's mental processes. He knew Holt didn't have the witnesses to probate Adelaide's will. He had expected Holt to grill Reg about them. He'd set himself to run interference for his skittish young heir — with objections to distract Holt's attention and side-bar cuts to draw his anger.

But now Holt had let Reg off the hook. Kane wasn't sure why. His edginess was directed not only at Holt but also at a tiny doubt inside himself.

Holt nodded pleasantly. "Thank you, Mr. Kane. That will save time."

Once again facing the court, Holt tried for the businesslike air of a lawyer on the routine matter of proving up an uncontested will.

"Your Honor," he said in a matter-of-fact tone, "the will you have there was written in its entirety by the testatrix. I'd like to introduce in evidence the machine on which she typed it." He reached for the battered portable.

Kane exploded out of his chair with a swoosh.

"Objection!" Kane thundered. He turned to Holt, sneering. "So that's the way you planned to prove up this will! You've got to have a witness!"

Holt tried to watch Kane and Reg at the same time. Like the old Statue-of-Liberty play, the surprise attack he planned depended on timing and deception. Reg looked off guard, smiling triumphantly as his lawyer hammered down the opposition.

Kane was relishing the moment with obvious satisfaction. It wasn't every day you could demonstrate your learning to most of Pinewood. He half faced the spectators as he made his argument to the judge.

"In order to prove up a will written by a decedent, the will itself . . . every word of it . . . has to be in decedent's handwriting. This will's typed. Even if Adelaide Bailey did type it, it can't be proved except by a witness who was there, saw her sign it, and signed it himself."

210

Judge Woodruff checked further debate with a rap of his gavel. "Objection sustained. Identifying the typing as decedent's would be immaterial, Mr. Lawson. We must have a witness to the will."

Holt shrugged. "Very well. I call Mr. Thomas Davenport."

From the door of the clerk's office a voice called, "Here."

Theodore Calhoun stepped forward. — That is, Holt had to assume it was Theodore. He'd defy anyone to tell him from Oliver.

Distinguished-looking in dark blue suit and maroon tie, Theodore made his way to the witness stand.

Watching carefully, Holt saw surprise, bewilderment hit Reg, who sat as though stupified.

Not so Kane. First, he shot a glance at Theodore; then studied Holt through narrowed eyes. His indecision, Holt knew, wasn't because he hadn't instantly seen the use Holt might make of a bogus Davenport. Rather it was that he couldn't believe Holt capable of anything so monstrous.

To help him make up his mind, Holt gave Kane a faint, mocking smile.

Kane's face flushed. The muscles of his jaws stood out, worked spasmodically. His hands began to tremble. He was, in that moment, the perfect picture of an attorney — outraged, incredulous — who finally faces the fact that his opponent is about to try to prove up a will with perjured testimony.

Holt sucked in a quick, shallow breath. He had to move fast now. Before Kane got his rage in hand. Before there could be any weighing of the pros and cons of the situation.

Turning quickly to his witness, Holt asked, "Are you the Thomas Davenport who witnessed the will of Adelaide Bailey in Hilma, Texas?"

Theodore Calhoun nodded. "I am."

Reg gasped.

Holt stole a look. Pretty Boy was whispering excitedly in Kane's ear.

Kane shook him off. The big lawyer sat hunched in his chair, the muscles of his neck corded. His eyes burned. But still he didn't move.

Holt walked to the bench and picked up the will. His palms were sweating. He rubbed his hands against his trousers . . . held the will with his finger tips so he wouldn't wet it.

Had Kane smelled the trap? Heart pounding, Holt handed the will to Theodore. "I ask you, is this the signature of Adelaide Bailey?"

"It is." Theodore's tone was matter-of-fact. Clearly a busy man willing to give of his time to do his civic duty. "I saw her sign it."

"That's a lie!" Reg's voice quavered.

Holt tensed; waited.

And now Kane, thundering:

"Perjury!"

It was commitment. Reg's break had triggered an explosion at last.

Some of the tension went out of Holt. Yet even as it did so, his excitement increased. So, he'd flushed his tiger. Next question: Could he make the kill?

Kane stalked forward to the judge's bench, wheeled and pointed an accusing finger at Holt. "How often shall this man be allowed to set up false witnesses? I tell you, Judge, I personally know this to be barefaced perjury."

"You don't personally know a damned thing about it," Holt snapped. "Either one of you."

The judge banged his gavel for order. But Reg scampered to Kane's side. Standing on tip-toe, he grasped the edge of

212

the bench and pushed his face as near the judge as he could.

"We saw the men who signed Aunt Adelaide's will," he babbled. He pointed to Theodore. "He's a fake!"

"That's the gospel truth!" Kane shook his head in vigorous agreement.

Holt wanted to get at Reg at once. Before Kane had some second guesses. But first he had to get Theodore off the stand without giving Kane a crack at him.

Swiftly, he stepped forward, shot an indignant look at Kane, and faced Judge Woodruff. "Your Honor, impeachment of the witness should have come on cross-examination. This attack is out of order. These personal accusations against me are unprecedented. I ask permission to interrupt my examination. To have Mr. Davenport stand aside until I clear this matter up."

Stern-faced, Judge Woodruff glared through his glassy left eye. "Mr. Lawson, I shall not only permit — I shall require that you do so! Bailiff, take Mr. Davenport into custody!"

Holt spun on Reg, observing with satisfaction that his victim-to-be had lost the triumphant smile of a few moments before. "I call Reginald Bailey to the stand," he snapped.

Judge Woodruff nodded stiff-necked affirmation. "You've been sworn, Mr. Bailey. Take the stand," he ordered. "We'll see what this is all about."

Reg walked hesitantly to the stand. His righteous indignation appeared to be waning. Holt paced restlessly, anxious to get at him.

With his hand on the gate to the witness box, Reg cast a last appealing look at his lawyer. Then he pushed his way through the aperture and slumped into the chair.

Holt crossed to a position between Kane and Reg, standing so that he blocked out any possible signals between them.

"You weren't there when your aunt signed her will, were

213

you?" he demanded.

Reg twisted in his chair. But Holt moved, too, so that Reg couldn't see around to Kane. At last he had Reg on the horns of the dilemma he'd planned!

If Reg hadn't been there when Adelaide signed her will, he couldn't swear positively this man hadn't witnessed it. If he had been there, he could expect the grilling from Holt that he'd been ducking.

"I object!" Matthew Kane was on his feet again, moving to a position directly in front of the judge's bench where Holt couldn't shut him out of Reg's view.

Holt put an impatient frown on his face. But inwardly he smiled and waited like a fisherman who feels the first nibble on his line.

Kane faced Reg as he stated his objection. "Even if Mr. Bailey was there, the will can't be proved by him. He wasn't one of the witnesses. The question's irrelevant and immaterial."

As an objection it was silly. Reg's presence was pertinent to the inquiry into the authenticity of Davenport. But as a message, Kane's objection was precise.

Holt watched Reggie's face clear. Now he had the coach's signal. Kane might as well have written him a note. "No choice except to show up this Davenport for a liar. Lawson can't prove the will by you. Just remember the answers I gave you to the questions he'll fire next."

Reg took a deep breath. "I was there when she signed the will," he said stubbornly.

"You saw the men sign as witnesses," Holt insisted.

Reggie studied the floor of the witness box for a moment. "Yeah, I guess so," he admitted.

Holt drew a deep breath of his own. "Thomas Davenport and Bruce Jennings?" he persisted.

"That's what they said their names were," Reggie's voice

214

went up to a higher pitch. "Anyway, it wasn't that guy you had up here!"

"That's all for this witness." Holt turned back to Judge Woodruff. "I call Mr. Matthew Kane. He hasn't been sworn."

For a moment Reggie sat limp. Then a look of relief came over his face. He shot out of the witness box as though the chair had blistered his behind.

Glaring through his cold, left eye, Judge Woodruff administered Matthew Kane a very solemn oath.

Kane seemed barely aware of it. Absently, he muttered, "I do." Frowning, he walked slowly toward the witness stand. Holt could read his thoughts. Why had Holt let Reg off? Why hadn't he tried to tear out of Reggie the identities of the witnesses to Adelaide's will? Surely he couldn't think Kane would be easier game.

Then Kane straightened his great shoulders and stepped determinedly into the witness box. Settling himself in the chair, he faced Holt. And a tiny smile at the corner of his mouth challenged his opponent to do his damnedest.

Holt didn't want Kane too thoughtful. He baited another attack. "You've made a serious charge against me," he declared.

"You've made a serious mistake," Kane retorted.

"You question the integrity of a man like Mr. Davenport . . ." Holt waved a hand toward Theodore, the picture of a man of substance in his new clothes, "and of a fellow lawyer, on the say-so of . . ."

He turned and threw a scornful glance at the bulgy figure at the counsel table. ". . . of Reggie?"

"No, I don't," Kane snapped. "I don't question your integrity. I deny it. And not on anybody's say-so. I was there!"

"You saw the men who . . ." Holt began.

"Look, get this through your head," Kane cut him off. "I

215

was there. I just happened to be in Hilma. Miss Bailey wanted a lawyer to see the will was properly executed. I saw the witnesses sign. Your 'Davenport' is a perjurer. You're guilty of subornation of perjury, and I can swear to it!"

Holt heard Burgess gasp.

Judge Woodruff's gavel cracked on the bench. That pale, impassive iris of his left eye fixed itself on Holt. "Is this true, Mr. Lawson?" he demanded.

That damned eye! Holt choked down his revulsion. "There's no such person as Thomas Davenport," he admitted. "Or Jennings. Kane ran in a couple of frauds so the will couldn't be probated."

"That's a red herring!" Kane jeered. "Reginald got a couple of men sitting in the lobby. You should have reviewed Miss Bailey's will during her lifetime."

There was an unnatural quiet in the courtroom. Holt looked up at the judge's bench. That ghastly, cadaverous left eye stared down unblinkingly. Holt congratulated himself that the days of the rack and thumbscrew were past.

"This is outrageous contempt of this court!" Judge Woodruff rasped. "Do you have anything to say before I sentence you?"

"Yes, your Honor." Holt grinned in spite of himself. "I ask that the will of Adelaide Bailey be admitted to probate."

A hissing noise swept the courtroom, the sound of many breaths sharply sucked in.

Matthew Kane grabbed the edge of the witness box and leaned forward. "You what . . .?"

Judge Woodruff swung around on his bench and cocked his right eyebrow.

Holt rummaged among the papers on the table and came up with a blue-backed document that he handed to the judge. "Here's a brief of the cases, your Honor. The rule is summarized in 44 Texas Jurisprudence on Wills, section 93."

Returning to the counsel table he picked up a thick volume and read, "If the witnesses to a will cannot be produced, the will can be probated by proof of two witnesses of the handwriting of the testatrix and of the persons who witnessed the will. When such testimony is produced, it is presumed the will was executed with all specified formalities."

Kane's eyes distended. Swinging out of the witness box, he made a dash for the bench and faced the judge.

"He hasn't produced a single witness! That's no evidence to probate a will on!" Kane pounded the heel of his right hand into the palm of his left. "All he's done is make an unsupported attack on my client and myself."

Holt spread his arms wide. "Your honor, Matthew Kane and Reginald Bailey just testified they were there and saw Adelaide Bailey and two witnesses sign her will. There couldn't be any better evidence of the handwriting of the testatrix and witnesses."

Someone in the rear of the room sniggered. Judge Woodruff gaveled for silence.

Kane rubbed his hand over his slack mouth. Then, pulling out a handkerchief, he mopped at his brow. "This is preposterous." His voice had lost its usual boom. "Lawson admits there're no such people as Davenport and Jennings. The names on the will are fictitious."

Holt glanced down at his copy of the brief he'd handed the judge. "You do something, lying about your name doesn't undo it. See 30B Texas Jurisprudence. Fictitious names don't invalidate their act of witnessing the will."

Someone burst out laughing, and all at once the men at the rear of the courtroom were cheering. A voice bolder than the rest whooped, "You tell 'em, Holt!"

Judge Woodruff didn't bother with his gavel. He cocked his head to the right and focused a fierce left-eyed stare on

217

the knot of men. The noise died suddenly. In the dead quiet Holt could hear Kane's heavy breathing.

Judge Woodruff spent a moment flipping the pages of Holt's brief. Then he reached for his docket sheet and scribbled on it.

"Glad to have the authorities with me," he said with a frosty smile. "The will of Adelaide Bailey is admitted to probate. Holt Lawson appointed executor."

The crowd remained quiet. The kind of tense quiet of a well-trained dog quivering to spring at the word of release.

Holt dropped into his chair, puffed his lips and let out a long breath. He'd pulled it off. He'd be handling Adelaide's affairs. But from behind bars?

Judge Woodruff gave Kane a left-eyed glare. "Never bumped into a cuter way of trying to suppress a will. But it happened outside my jurisdiction. We'll have to see what the State Bar says of your ethics."

Then the diminutive judge swung back to Holt. Holt stood, faced the glint of that large, impassive, staring left eye.

Judge Woodruff hefted his gavel thoughtfully. "On the other hand, Mr. Lawson, I do have jurisdiction of you. Your actions took place in my court."

The judge's hesitation encouraged Holt. It wasn't to be the thumbscrew or the rack! Perhaps only a few strokes of the whip and disbarment.

"I understand your motives . . ." Judge Woodruff seemed to be talking to himself. He pinched his lower lip between the thumb and forefinger of his left hand. The fingers of his right hand drummed slowly on the bench. Then he shook his head, and his mouth tightened into a thin, determined line. "But technically, it's still perjury."

"Technically, it never was perjury." Holt grabbed a book from the table, moved nearer the judge's bench and that awful eye, and then half turned. "Will Theodore and Oliver

Calhoun come up here?" he called.

Theodore got up from a chair next to the desk of the bailiff. Oliver emerged from the court clerk's office and joined him. Together, the two tall, lanky, Lincolnesque duplicates ambled forward.

Holt opened the book and handed it to the judge. "Perjury in a legal proceeding is defined as the giving of false testimony under oath."

Reading, Judge Woodruff nodded agreement.

Holt turned to the two Calhouns. "Now Oliver Calhoun..." He paused uncertainly. Oliver raised an identifying hand.

"Oliver Calhoun," Holt continued, "was under oath. But Oliver Calhoun gave no testimony, false or otherwise. It was Theodore Calhoun..."

Theodore acknowledged his curtain call with a bow.

"... Theodore Calhoun who gave the testimony that proved so stimulating to the tongues of Messrs. Kane and Bailey. And Theodore Calhoun was not under oath."

Judge Woodruff re-read the definition Holt had handed up to him. Then he leaned back in his chair and again pinched his lower lip between thumb and forefinger.

"These men are no more than paid performers?" he demanded.

Holt shook his head in the affirmative. "That's all. I authored the whole thing."

Judge Woodruff turned to the Calhouns. Relieved, Holt saw that it was the good right eye which studied them.

A brief pause. Then the judge smiled thinly. "I take it," he said, "you artists were — I believe the expression is, 'at liberty' — when Mr. Lawson employed you for his little drama. Very well, I shall leave you in that condition."

Holt stepped back a couple of paces and leaned against the counsel table, feeling a little of the tenseness drain away

219

from him. At least he had the Calhouns, God bless 'em, off the hook.

The faint smile at the corner of the judge's mouth disappeared. He seemed glad to have found a way to dispose of the nonentities and get back to the real culprit. Swinging his head to the right, he glared through his pale, cold left eye.

Holt straightened up and steeled himself.

"Now for you, Mr. Lawson," the judge grated. "I believe I've considered all the implications of your conduct. I'm ready to pass sentence. That sentence is . . . I hereby require you to act as my counsel if I ever get into trouble!"

Holt blinked, gasped. There was a twinkle in that glassy eye! He felt his mouth hanging open and closed it.

Chuckling, Judge Woodruff banged his gavel. "Court's dismissed," he announced and hied himself to his chambers.

For a moment there was utter silence in the courtroom. Then, released, the men at the back shouted a cheer. Almost immediately there was an echo from outside. The V-for-victory signal had been sent and received.

The crowd surged forward with so much the enthusiasm of victorious fans spilling out onto the gridiron that Holt braced himself lest some try to hoist him to their shoulders.

But underlying their exuberance he sensed a deep gratitude that touched him and made it impossible for him to break away from their awkward attempts to express it.

So it was that he found himself cut off from Burgess and Miss Phoebe. Over the men's shoulders he watched his efficient secretary gather his papers, stow them in his briefcase, and steer her older companion through the knot of sympathizers to the exist.

Still father off, he saw the occupants of the jury box make their way around the mob and out of the courtroom.

Then Connie was at his side. She all but threw her arms around him, and her eyes sparkled. "Holt," she exulted, "you're fantastic!"

He grinned and gave her a quick hug. "It was nothing that any sneaky quarterback couldn't have dreamed up," he assured her.

Then Connie put her hand on his arm. The tone of her voice suddenly turned wretched, urgent. "I've got to talk to you, Holt," she said.

Concerned, Holt directed an all-inclusive "excuse me" to the men surrounding him. Taking Connie's elbow, he guided her to the alcove between the jury box and the wall enclosing the judge's chambers.

Connie faced him. Her chin began to tremble. Tears formed in her eyes, giving them a different sparkle. She took a half step forward and steadied herself against him.

"Holt, Dad's not supposed to know, but he managed to find out . . . the bank examiners are coming . . . maybe even today. Oh, Holt, help me!"

For a moment, Holt held back. Old man Townsend hadn't earned any favors from him. But then the sight of Connie in her abject misery washed away his resentment. He wanted to take her in his arms and comfort her but, aware of the lingering spectators, he covered her hand with his and gave a reassuring squeeze.

He nodded toward the jury room in the back of the chamber. "Get hold of Reg and have him meet me in there."

"You can . . . you will help us, won't you, Holt?" Connie pleaded.

Holt released her hand and stepped back. "Go use the tears on Reg," he advised. "If he'll cooperate, I'll save your dad's skin."

Chapter 20

As soon as he could, Holt broke loose from the handshaking and congratulations, gathered up the briefcase Burgess had readied, and hurried back to the room where juries held their deliberations.

Reg and Kane were both waiting. Holt frowned at Kane, then reminded himself that the presence of Reg's attorney was ethically correct.

Kane hunched in a chair at one end of the long conference table that dominated the room. The giant figure seemed to have withered. Kane's string tie had come loose. The long gray mane that always lay in just-so senatorial fashion hung dishevelled.

Holt felt a funny prickle along his spine. Sloppiness on Kane was unnatural, grotesque.

Reg sat with his arm chair tilted back against the wall and his feet on the center table. He put forth no greeting — just a glum look.

Holt threw his briefcase on the table and sat on its edge facing Reg. "I thought you'd be more cordial to the guy that just saved you a half million bucks."

Reg started. "How'd you save me a half million?"

Holt glanced down the table. "Kane's fee. Didn't his contingent fee call for a half of what he won? Well, he didn't

223

win anything."

Kane glared, began to breathe hard.

Reg rubbed his chin. "I don't know . . . Kane probably covered that."

"It doesn't make any difference what you signed." Holt gave a short laugh. "Adelaide's estate goes into a spendthrift trust. Nothing you've signed . . . none of your creditors . . . can touch it."

Reg shot an uneasy glance at Kane. Kane's mouth worked.

"You two are getting chummy in a hurry," he rasped in a taut, ugly voice. "Do you think you're going to cut me out?"

"I know I am," Holt retorted. "Adelaide named me Reg's wet nurse, and I aim to do my job."

Holt turned to Reg. That young man's pretty face had lost a little of its glumness, and he appeared to be giving Holt a fresh appraisal.

Holt smiled. "Connie says you want to help her dad out of the spot he's in."

"Damned right." Reg nodded his head vigorously. "Show me where to get fifty thousand bucks, and we'll put it back in the bank's till."

Holt felt kindlier toward Reg than he had at any time since their teens. The other's eagerness to help the Townsends was washing away a lot of accumulated hostility.

"I can buy your stock in Adelaide's Bakeries," Holt said. "It's worth over fifty thousand. But I can't if you appeal Woodruff's order appointing me executor. If you do, I'll have no authority until the District Court handles the appeal."

"We'll appeal, by God!" Kane lurched forward, supporting himself against the table. He uttered his pronouncement in gasps. "I've worked — and planned — and waited for this too long — to be done out of it now."

"You'd lose. Half of Pinewood heard the evidence," Holt

said curtly. He turned back to Reg and grinned. "Anyway, you'd probably need a new lawyer. Woodruff's going to see this gentleman disbarred."

The veins in Kane's neck corded. A trickle of spit dripped down his chin. Repelled, Holt averted his glance.

Reg looked momentarily happy, then his face lost its animation, and he snapped his fingers. "Oh, hell! I signed that stock over to Fox."

Holt's estimate of Adelaide's precious nephew continued upward. "A gambling debt's not legal consideration," he pointed out. "The transfer wasn't valid."

"But I gave Fox the stock certificate. Don't you need it?"

"Well, yes." Holt made a wry face at the memory of the episode in Fox's office. He gestured toward his briefcase. "It's there. Your wet nurse latched onto it for you."

Reg sat silent for a few moments, seeming to let all the news sink in. Then his plump, prettish face formed into a happier expression than Holt had seen on it in months, and he got to his feet. "Well, what are we waiting for? Let's get over to the bank!"

Holt pushed up from his perch on the table.

"No!" Kane thundered.

Holt and Reg turned simultaneously.

Kane's eyes had a wild gleam to them, and they fixed on Reg. The big man struggled to his feet and planted both hands on the table to support himself.

"Thou wilt not deal falsely with me." Kane started for Reg. Leaning heavily on the table, he walked his hands along the edge, using them to support and drag his body. His breath came in short, labored gasps that almost prevented speech. "Ye are full . . . of hypocrisy . . . Yet will I be . . . avenged of you . . ."

Reg let out a gasp. His girlish lips flopped open.

225

Holt tensed, moved to put himself between Reg and this madman.

But Kane stopped, clutched his chest with his right hand and fell heavily into an empty chair.

"Kane," Holt began, "If this is more of your theatrics . . ."

But Kane's eyes glazed and rolled upward. His face paled and broke out in a profuse sweat. Exactly as Adelaide's had done just before she died.

Holt spun about and shoved the solid door open. The court bailiff was lounging at the entrance to the clerk's office.

"Mr. Meade!" Holt shouted. "Get George White over here with some oxygen. And call Doc Hardwick. Looks like Kane's having a real heart attack!"

Then he hurried back into the jury room. Reg had Kane's vial of pills opened and was poking one under the stricken man's tongue. Holt twisted the corner of his mouth upward mirthlessly.

"That's not going to help, Reg," Holt said. "Saccharin didn't save Adelaide. Let him lie down."

But at that instant, Kane groaned and fell to the floor.

Chapter 21

Kane was dead. It took Dr. Hardwick only a moment to confirm it. The doctor refused to engage in speculation as to whether Kane's coronary thrombosis might have developed from an angina attack which nitroglycerin would have relieved.

"In the first place," he said, "I'd be guessing. In the second place, we never fill in the 'cause' blank on a death certificate with 'poetic justice' or 'reaped where he had sown'."

The ambulance siren had brought a goodly crowd to the courtroom, including Connie and Burgess. Holt drew aside and didn't hover as the Whites repeated with Kane's body the procedure they had followed with Adelaide's. Holt felt no particular emotion, except a grudging admiration for the way Kane had still been fighting, even as he went down.

Burgess left the group and came to where Holt stood. Connie and Reg followed closely.

Holt handed Burgess his briefcase. "The file has everything you need. Fix up the order probating the will, executor's oath, and call the insurance agency to make my bond."

Connie's eyebrows drew together in a worried frown. "Can't the technicalities wait, Holt? We've got to get over to the bank."

"I'm coming," Holt said sharply. They weren't just technicalities. An executor had no authority whatsoever until he filed his oath and bond. Already he was taking a chance for Connie, and it annoyed him to have it so unappreciated.

Burgess seemed to sense the situation. "Holt, you can't do anything at the bank without giving them copies of the order. And you know how Woodruff double-checks the dates on . . ."

Connie took a restless step toward the door.

Holt gripped Burgess's arm and started her for the exit. "Just get everything ready. I'll see that it's signed and filed today," he assured her.

Trailing Connie and Reg, Burgess's other objection recurred to Holt, and he grinned crookedly. Small worry that Townsend would insist on a copy of the court order as a condition to transferring the funds that would cover up his embezzlement.

At the bank, Holt raced through the several transactions that got Townsend's accounts in good enough shape for the old boy to be able to look the bank examiners in the face. Then he hurried to his office and back to Judge Woodruff's chambers to get his oath and bond approved and his position as Adelaide's legal representative nailed down.

It was a wearing afternoon. By the time he was done, Holt was ready to go home and have a shower and a drink before Connie came.

But he wanted to do some thinking about Connie. The incident in the courtroom had worked on him. Not that he wanted any woman interfering in his business. But, perversely, he would have preferred that Connie had shown some interest in what risk he ran in writing a check for fifty thousand on Adelaide's account before he had any authority to do so. Maybe it was time to analyze Connie's motives all through the fight for the Bailey fortune.

So he forced himself back to his office where he wouldn't have a highball to help him dismiss Connie's actions from his mind too easily.

The neatness of Burgess's desk told him she had left. On the table in his private sanctum lay items that had accumulated in the case . . . corporate records, Adelaide's beat-up portable typewriter, the miscellaneous junk he'd kept from her purse. Holt passed by the miscellany and relaxed in his desk chair.

Connie's picture held a central position on the desk top. In radiant color, it portrayed a woman of beauty, intelligence, and decency.

That was the girl he wanted. But he didn't want the flesh-and-blood Connie if she cared only for the money and power he could now bring to their marriage.

He started to pace again, then paused at the table with its crop of junk. Adelaide's battered old portable typewriter sat on top of the pile of corporation books. Holt studied it thoughtfully.

If he loved Connie, wasn't there something indecent about laying a trap for her? He answered his question with action. Lugging the ancient machine to his desk, he ran a sheet of paper into the roller, blocked the view of Connie's picture with a book, and began to peck away at the keys.

A little before six, he swung his station wagon into his drive and pulled up to the back door. Connie's sports car wasn't there yet.

Holt got out and stretched.

Now Snubby burst through the canvas flap that covered his entrance. Yipping and prancing, he leaped toward Holt's arms as far as his short legs would project.

Holt picked the little dog up and roughed his fur. "I hate to do this, fellow," he said, "but one of your scraps with Connie would just complicate matters." Then, carrying the Peke onto the porch, he pushed him under the flap again and blocked the small entrance with a box.

Snubby spent a few minutes in indignant barking. Watching the performance through a slit in the blind, Holt couldn't help chuckling, although he felt like a heel for giving his furry friend the brush-off.

Finally Snubby stalked away. Holt went into the living room, closed the venetian blinds and turned on the table lamp.

In the semi-gloom, anything under the lamp would be spotlighted. Taking a typed page from his coat, Holt put it in an envelope of Adelaide's and centered it in the lamplight.

The low growl of a lot of well-harnessed horsepower passed outside the window. By the time he reached the back porch, he found Connie had already parked her stream-lined sports car next to the station wagon.

Hastily, Holt pushed the screen door open. Looking cool and chic, Connie came briskly up the back stairs and entered. A breath of provocative fragrance eddied in her wake. Holt followed her, admiring the sway of her hips as she crossed the kitchen. It was an effect, he noted, in no small measure enhanced by her ivory white peasant dress, tight at the waist, loose at breast and skirt.

In front of the old-fashioned sink, she stopped, turned and leaned back. As she moved, the light caught her copper hair and the coppery cloth that made a design in her blouse.

"Holt, you don't know what you did for my morale this afternoon." She stretched her hands toward the ceiling, and her eyes brightened. "Let's make merry!"

Connie had a way of exhilerating him. Holt laughed. "You take the cupboard, and I'll take the ice box!"

She did. Scotch and sparkling water followed.

In his turn, Holt pulled an ice tray from the refrigerator, flipped ice cubes out of the rubber divider and popped them into the glasses. Already he was relishing the tang of the drink and the flavor of Connie's kisses.

Then he remembered the envelope he'd left on the living room table. He hesitated, holding the empty ice tray.

Connie brushed his lips with hers. "Don't go solemn again, Holt." Her eyes smiled at him.

Her gaiety was catching. "Okay," Holt said. "Fix the drinks."

By the time he'd refilled the tray and put it back in the refrigerator, Connie was holding a highball out to him. Holt took it and put his other arm around her waist. Together they walked to the front room. At each step her hip, round and firm, swayed against his thigh.

Now, kicking the sandals from her small feet, Connie sat on the divan. Holt joined her. Neither of them said anything while they sipped their Scotch.

Then the glasses were empty, set aside. Leaning back, Holt savored the moment. The alcohol had stimulated his physical consciousness of Connie.

Turning, Holt pulled her to him.

Connie's head brushed against the cushions, marring the perfection of her hairdo. It made her look more yielding. Holt put his hand behind her head and disordered the copper hair still more, completely destroying the glacial, just-so look. Then he kissed her.

At once she returned his kiss, blowing her warm breath into his mouth. Her fingers touched the hollow behind his ear.

Holt tightened his arm around her waist. Connie's body pressed against him with a small thrilling quiver.

"Start this zipper for me, Holt," she said, "and then go

231

get me another drink."

Holt pushed up off the couch. Whatever her motives, Connie sure as hell roused his desire.

He found the tab and pulled. The peasant frock opened to Connie's hips, revealing the smooth, tanned perfection of her back.

He slipped his hands inside the dress. What would he find this time? The girdle? The play pants? The bikini?

He found nothing. Absolutely nothing but warm flesh.

Encircling her, he covered her firm rounded stomach with his hands.

Connie leaned back, nestling her body against him. Holt began to move his hands in gentle, pressing circles across her front and felt the hard swell, the quick rise and fall, of her young breasts.

Connie caught his wrists and hugged his hands against her. Flushed with desire, he clasped her to him and tried to shrug her dress over her arms. It twisted tighter. Turning her head back, she gave him a loose, passionate kiss. "I'll get the dress off, you ape," she said. "But I could use that drink when I do."

Holt bit the lobe of her ear gently and let her go. As he headed for the kitchen, he saw the envelope he'd put on the table spotlighted beneath the lamp.

He hesitated. Today Connie'd found out at long last that it would be Holt who'd control Adelaide's fortune. And, presto, the impregnable girdle had vanished.

Holt shook his head. Now he was unwilling to chance Connie's not seeing the envelope. He pointed to it.

"I've got to talk to you about that," he said.

And so to the kitchen. You think too much, he told himself, and made his drink extra strong.

Back to the front room again.

Connie stood by the table, reading the page from the

envelope. She'd only got as far as slipping her dress off one shoulder. Now, at Holt's approach, she tugged it back on.

Holt put her drink on the table by the empty envelope. The lamp highlighted Connie's clean-cut features.

In the flesh, Connie looked just like the portrait on Holt's desk . . . like the picture of her he'd drawn for himself. Now he watched for her reaction to the paper in her hand . . . the reaction that would tell him how accurately these images reflected Connie's character.

Then Connie turned to him, flourishing the page of typing. "What is this, Holt?"

Momentarily Holt hesitated. But only momentarily. He had to have done with his doubts.

"It's a codicil to Adelaide's will," he answered. "I found it at her office the other day."

"Holt, this says Reg and the bank are to be co-trustees with you. What does that mean?"

"It means I expect your dad to stick with me." He took her hand and smiled. "I guess we can count on that."

"You mean Reg and he could out-vote you?"

"Hell, yes!" Holt gave a snort of disgust. "I guess Adelaide thought I sounded too sour on her precious nephew. She really messed things up!"

"You mean by voting together, Reg and Dad could manage to get hold of big chunks of cash — like you did today?"

Holt increased his pressure on Connie's hand. "Connie, if you don't keep your dad on our side, they could fire me, sell the plant, and dream up a dozen reasons to dish out the dough to Reg. You and I'd be in a hell of a way."

Connie freed her hand and picked up her drink. Holt noticed she kept the codicil clutched tightly and reached for the drink with her free hand. Her face told him nothing. Nor did she speak, though she'd had plenty of time to say, "Burn

233

the thing" or "Dad'll be okay, Holt."

Seconds, ticking by. Then, abruptly, Connie took a long pull at her drink. When she set the glass down, it was with a click of decision. Reaching behind her, she zipped her dress closed.

A sort of hollow, heavy sensation formed in Holt's stomach. He wanted to cry out "It's a forgery, kid. Don't sucker for it!" But he kept his mouth shut and felt the tight, humorless grin on his face.

Connie put the paper back in its envelope and stuck it down the front of her dress. "I *am* fond of you, Holt," she said. "But I guess I'm more like Ming than Snubby."

"That sounds like a preamble to something."

"I want you to understand. That dog would follow you from stable to sty." Connie's gesture was all female. "Well, Ming loves me. But neither love nor sex will budge a cat for long from the spot where she's found security."

"And you're like that?"

Connie smiled lazily at him and nodded. In the semidark, her eyes did look rather like Ming's. "Security to Ming is a place," she said. "To me, it's money."

Holt took a stiff drink. It didn't help. Connie hadn't even had to think twice about choosing between him and a well-lined purse.

"I suppose now you'll set your cap for 'dear cousin' Reg," he said bitterly.

Connie laughed out loud. "Holt, you're too sweet. Reg has signed us in as 'Mr. and Mrs.' so often he wouldn't feel natural any other way."

Holt put his drink on the table. He ached to slap the smile from Connie's face.

In a way, he did.

"You really don't have to keep that masterpiece of mine pressed to your breast," he jibed. "I'll lend you Adelaide's portable any time, and you can type as many as you like."

That took the smile from her face. She put her hand to her bosom where she'd stuck the paper. "Adelaide didn't write this!"

Holt pasted a smirk on his face. Inside he felt as though a hot wind had dried up all his vital fluids. "That's right, precious . . . it was nothing any sneaky quarterback couldn't have dreamed up."

Connie pulled the page out, crumpled it, and threw it on the floor. Breathing in angry little gasps, she glared at him. Holt felt his lips twist in a sardonic smile. Connie had looked so worldly-wise when she was letting him know how she'd played him along. Now that she realized two could bait a trap, her gloss of superciliousness had faded.

He picked up his drink and turned away. "Connie," he suggested, "why don't you get the hell out of here?"

For a long moment Connie stood as if carved in ice. Then she took two steps toward the kitchen. Stopped. Turned back.

And, as though instinctively, she used a gesture that trollops have used since time immemorial.

She spit at Holt and stalked out of the room.

The back door slammed violently. Connie was gone. Holt eyed the scrap of paper she'd crumpled and thrown to the floor. His forgery had worked beautifully. He'd been oh so damned clever.

The sight of the paper disgusted him. He gave it a kick that sent it across the room. Then, picking up his glass, he marched purposefully into the kitchen. He wanted nothing so much as to blank out.

Snubby was in the kitchen investigating his pan. Apparently he'd made prompt use of Connie's exit to get back in the house.

Holt poured some feed into Snubby's bowl. "You're a great judge of character," Holt observed, "and it's a damn good thing for you that you can't tell me so."

Then he double-shot his drink, returned to the living room and sank on the couch.

How long he lay there he didn't know. A sense of complete aloneness engulfed him. Adelaide had been a third parent, her affairs the bulk of his daily work. She was dead. Burgess had become his right arm in the office and courtroom. She was leaving. He'd thought of Connie as the keystone of a real home and family. Now she'd slammed the door on those plans and dreams.

From time to time he sipped doggedly at his drink. Not that he really wanted it. But he did want to turn off the torture.

He knew he had to be pooped after the day he'd been through. He'd doze if only he could slow down the wheels spinning in his head. If he could stop thinking about Connie. But it didn't help to keep telling himself she was a bitch. He'd still lost the woman he'd imagined her to be.

Gradually a warm glow came over him. Adelaide and Burgess and Connie came in arm in arm and told him everything was all right and he could sleep.

But then Adelaide began poking Connie with her cane. Connie pulled a stilletto from her garter and started for Adelaide. Burgess stepped in between and flattened her hands into twin hatchets. Only it wasn't Burgess. It was Kane, and he was stalking Holt.

Holt tried to yell a warning, but he couldn't get the sound out of his throat. He grabbed Kane's arm and hung on.

Opening his eyes, he found himself on the sofa in his living room with a death grip on the pillows.

He pulled himself up and looked at his watch. Ten o'clock. It was no surprise to find he'd slept a couple of hours. He could feel the recharge in his body's batteries.

Across the room, Snubby, too, roused, cocked his ears, got down from the chair in which he'd been lying, and came over.

Holt reached down to scratch his dog behind the ears. "What'll we do, boy?" he asked. "I'm not going to sit around here moping."

A forty minute drive would take him to a wet county where he could find a beer joint and passably wicked companions. But for some reason the idea didn't hit him right.

Finally, for lack of any better inspiration, he went to the banisters and got down Snubby's leash. "C'mon boy. Let's take a walk."

Snubby made appropriately enthusiastic noises. Chuckling, Holt snapped the leash to the Peke's collar and allowed himself to be tugged through the front door and down the walk.

A full moon made the tall pine in the front yard a study of shimmering light against pools of shade.

Holt grimaced. It was a night to have your girl in your arms. So he'd spend it walking his dog.

At the sidewalk Holt paused, looked down Elm toward town, then up the street toward the homes of Burgess, Adelaide, and Connie.

Obviously, toward town was the sensible direction for any man out to avoid bleak memories.

But when he moved off down the dark tree-lined sidewalk, Holt found both himself and Snubby starting out Elm as if drawn by a magnet.

Dashing back and forth on his short legs, Snubby smelled out the day's news. Holt realized the Peke's nose was telling him who had been that way, with whom, and who followed. Just like humans' gossip columns about what movie star was trifling on which of her mates with whose husband.

Holt couldn't help but grin at the thought in spite of himself. Getting out of the house had helped. There was a pleasant coolness to the night air. He felt much improved.

All at once, Snubby stopped his circling and crisscrossing. His pull took on direction.

Holt snapped out of his musing. Snubby was tugging to go up the sidewalk to Burgess's house.

Kneeling, Holt pulled small-fry to him. "Easy, boy. It's too late for calling."

For answer, Snubby whined eagerly and pushed with his hind feet to be off.

Holt wondered if subconsciously he'd come this way with Snubby because it carried him closer to Burgess.

Burgess, who'd eased things for him when Adelaide died.

Burgess, who'd come panting into his house, jack handle in hand, to share whatever danger he'd walked into when he'd thought he had some henchman of Fox's cornered.

Burgess, who'd stood staunchly by when it appeared he'd lost lawsuit, reputation, everything.

Holt's throat tightened.

"You can't go barging in this late, fellow," he told Snubby again, huskily. But already he was unsnapping the leash.

Snubby dashed up the walk, negotiated the steep front steps with a sort of see-saw movement, and scratched at the front door.

The door opened. Burgess stood silhouetted against the light from inside the house. Stooping, she scooped Snubby up in her arms and stepped back inside. The door swung closed.

And here Holt stood. A peeping Tom to any neighbor who spotted him. While inside Snubby lay snug in Burgess's arms.

238

What was it Burgess had said when she'd pulled away from him in the courtroom? "I haven't the slightest desire to be a stand-in for your dear little Connie."

Now he knew why he had come this way. Once again Burgess was standing by when he needed her. Already thoughts of her were crowding into the void Connie had left. Like a rightful claimant coming into her own upon the ouster of the pretender.

Absently he slapped Snubby's leash against his thigh and felt the sting of the metal snap that fastened to Snubby's collar. He fingered it thoughtfully, eyeing the door where Snubby had disappeared.

Then he felt a smile tug at the corners of his mouth. He started up the walk toward Burgess's door.

Snubby's empty leash should do for an excuse to pop in. Even if the real emptiness was inside himself.

And then perhaps, some day when Burgess was sure, very sure, that for him there was no one else, again she'd come into his arms. Perhaps.

Perhaps, hell. There hadn't been any perhaps in the way Snubby went about maneuvering himself into Burgess's embrace.

Why, then, shouldn't Snubby's uncomplicated approach work for people, too?

Well, there was one sure way to find out.

Holt took the steps to the porch two at a time and pressed the door bell firmly.

THE END